"We need to get a few things straight, Ray Clyde." Ginger kept her voice low.

"What is it we need to get straight?" Ray asked.

"These two little girls are precious to me," she said quietly. "They don't need to be used as pawns so you can try to make amends with me."

There was a slight hesitation, then, "You know better." His voice chided but remained gentle, maybe a little sad. "Let's be honest with one another for a moment. You feel you need to place some distance between the two of us on this trip, and so you must make sure I don't bond with Lucy or Brittany."

"You have a problem with that?" she asked.

"I do. A considerable amount as a matter of fact."

Ginger shifted in her seat. No one else had quite the same knack of rendering her speechless like he did.

Books by Hannah Alexander

Love Inspired Suspense	Steeple Hill Single Title
Note of Peril #1	*Hideaway*
Under Suspicion #25	*Safe Haven*
Death Benefits #60	*Last Resort*
	Fair Warning
	Grave Risk

HANNAH ALEXANDER

is the pseudonym of husband-and-wife writing team Cheryl and Mel Hodde (pronounced Hoddee). When they first met, Mel had just begun his new job as an E.R. doctor in Cheryl's hometown, and Cheryl was working on a novel. Cheryl's matchmaking pastor set them up on an unexpected blind date at a local restaurant. Surprised by the sneak attack, Cheryl blurted the first thing that occurred to her, "You're a doctor? Could you help me paralyze someone?" Mel was shocked. "Only temporarily, of course," she explained when she saw his expression. "And only fictitiously. I'm writing a novel."

They began brainstorming immediately. Eighteen months later they were married, and the novels they set in fictitious Ozark towns began to sell. The first novel in the Hideaway series, published in the Steeple Hill Single Title program, won a prestigious Christy Award for Best Romance in 2004.

HANNAH ALEXANDER
Death Benefits

Steeple
Hill®

Published by Steeple Hill Books™

STEEPLE HILL BOOKS

Steeple
Hill®

ISBN-13: 978-0-373-44250-8
ISBN-10:   0-373-44250-5

DEATH BENEFITS

Copyright © 2007 by Hannah Alexander

www.SteepleHill.com

Printed in U.S.A.

Trust in the Lord with all your heart, and lean not on your own understanding. In all your ways submit to Him, and He will make your paths straight.

—*Proverbs* 3:5–6

With thanks to Ray and Clydene Brown, real, live heroes who were there for us in our time of need.

ONE

On New Year's Eve, Lucy Jameson dreamed she saw her dead mama's face in the fire. Mama had a pretty face, with eyes the color of sunshine through leaves, eyes that filled with love when she smiled. That was what Lucy missed the most about her—the smile, the love.

Mama didn't always smile, though.

In the fire, her eyes looked scary, and her mouth moved as if she might be shouting—though no sound came from her lips. She acted this way when she needed to get high. Soon, if she got high, she'd be happy for a few days.

Lucy wasn't supposed to know about these things, because she was only eight and a half. Some kids just knew, whether they were supposed to or not.

Mama stepped out of the fire and came toward Lucy, her hands black and smoking. Her feet burned into the wooden floor, spreading flames with every footstep.

Lucy gasped and sat up in bed, trying to scream as her eyes flew open in the dark. The sound came from her mouth like the chirp of a cricket. She knew it was her own voice; there weren't any crickets outside the window the week after Christmas in Hideaway, Missouri.

She hated these dreams worst of all. They made her remember the bad times, when her mother was scary-mad, when she slapped and screamed at Lucy and Brittany and called them nasty names. That was when Mama hated them.

"Sissy?"

Lucy winced at Brittany's frightened voice. "I'm here."

"What was that noise?"

"It's okay, it was me." Good thing she sounded normal again, not like the screechy cry from her dream.

There was a whisper of covers, then a thud of bare feet as Brittany dropped from her own bed and crossed to Lucy's.

She climbed up beside Lucy without asking permission.

Lucy pulled the blankets back and helped her settle under them. Even though Brittany kicked the covers off, and sometimes even snored, Lucy didn't mind. Much. Brittany couldn't help it, she was only five. She wouldn't be six until February.

Brittany squirmed close, right into Lucy's face. *Eeww!* Her breath stank.

"Did you have another bad dream?"

"Guess so." Lucy protected her nose with a handful of blanket.

"Was it about Mama again?"

Why did Aunt Ginger's spaghetti make their breath smell like this?

Brittany tugged at Lucy's arm. "Huh? Was it?"

"Yes," Lucy said. "Now be quiet or everybody will

wake up and nobody'll get back to sleep and we'll be tired all day tomorrow."

Brittany shifted…settled…shifted…settled, then snuggled close to Lucy's side. "Tomorrow's New Year's Day. Mama used to let us stay up until midnight on New Year's Eve."

"But we never got up early on New Year's Day to catch a plane to Hawaii when Mama was alive."

Brittany sighed. "No."

"You'll want to be awake for the airplane ride, so go back to sleep." They'd never flown.

"I don't know if I can sleep now. You scared me awake." Still, she yawned.

Lucy felt Brittany's teddy bear Chuckles being squeezed between them, his soft fur comforting as it had always been when they were alone at home, when Mom had been out somewhere in the night.

Lucy rubbed Brittany's head with gentle strokes and waited until her breathing grew deeper. Even when Brittany said she couldn't sleep, she always did.

"A dream," Lucy whispered to herself, remembering the angry face of her mother. "She's dead. It's okay now. She's dead." And then she cried, hating herself for saying that.

Willow Traynor was going to become their new mother next week. She wouldn't do the things Mama did, because she'd never done them.

Willow didn't look anything like Mama—Mama was pretty—but Willow was gentle, and when she spent time with Lucy and Brittany, it was as if she really wanted to be with them. She never yelled, and she hugged them a lot. She didn't take drugs, and she never slapped them. Willow made Lucy feel special.

As soon as Graham and Willow got married and everyone got home from the honeymoon, then Willow would move in here with Lucy and Brittany and Graham. Then, the week after that, the adoption would be final, and they would be a family.

Graham and Willow were going to be the most wonderful mother and father in the world. Lucy knew she could learn to feel safe with them.

She glanced across the room and barely saw the outline of Brittany's bed, the pile of blankets looking like a jumble of little hills in the moonlight.

Brittany had her own bedroom in this house, but even after all these months, Lucy and Brittany wanted to stay together. The same people who said Lucy was too mature for an eight-and-a-half-year-old couldn't believe Brittany was almost six. She was small for her age.

Light came in under the door, and it was brighter than the night-light, so that meant someone was up.

The surface of the lake, down the hill from the big log house where they lived, reflected lights from the boys' ranch on the other shore, where Blaze Farmer lived.

Lucy loved Blaze. When she grew up, she was going to marry him.

On any other night, if the lights were on at the ranch, it meant that it wasn't midnight yet. The boys all had to be in bed by eleven, even Blaze, who helped with the younger boys when he wasn't working at the clinic or in college. Tonight, all the boys got to stay up late because of New Year's Eve.

Lucy realized, since she'd heard no footsteps rushing down the hallway, that her cries from the nightmare hadn't been loud enough to be heard through the house. Sometimes, she screamed loud enough to wake Aunt Ginger or Graham. Then Aunt Ginger would place Brittany in bed with Lucy, and spend the rest of the night in Brittany's bed. She'd done that a few times since Mama died last spring.

Aunt Ginger said Lucy had never had the chance to be a child, and that she should learn to be one now. Lucy didn't know what she meant.

Sometimes, when Lucy woke up from a bad dream and couldn't stop shaking, she'd creep down the dim corridor to Aunt Ginger's room. She never made any noise, but sat on the floor in the corner, listening to Ginger breathing…sometimes snuggling into the clothes Ginger'd tossed off when she changed into her pajamas. The smell of Aunt Ginger made her feel safe.

Lucy would miss Aunt Ginger when she moved out.

Tonight wasn't a good night to wake her up, but if someone was already up anyway…

With slow, careful movements, Lucy pushed the covers back and slid to the floor. Had to be quiet. Brittany shouldn't wake up again. If she did, she might never get back to sleep.

Lucy opened the door, holding her breath. No sound came from the bed. She crept out into the hallway, but the telephone rang in the front room. She stopped, startled, then glanced back at her sister. No movement.

Who could be calling at this time of night?

* * *

Ginger Carpenter reached for the cordless phone beside her chair in the great room of her brother's lodge—that was how she would have to think of it from now on. No longer home. This would be her last night here.

Curious about who might be calling to wish them Happy New Year, she gave one final, longing glance toward the glow of the full winter moon over the lake.

She would miss this place. After the wedding in Hawaii, Ginger would move into Willow's condo off Lakeshore Drive. It was situated in a nice area, but it wouldn't have what Graham's roomy log house had—two little girls who had taken up so much of her time…and her heart…for the past nine months.

She answered the phone, glancing at the caller ID. It was blocked. "Yes."

"Ginger Carpenter, that you?" came a deep, gravelly voice that she was too tired to recognize.

"That's right."

"Larry Bager here."

Oh. Of course. How could she have forgotten that extremely masculine voice? Larry. Mr. Tough Guy himself. "Why is an undercover investigator calling here at this time of night?"

"I have to clue you and Graham in on some things."

"What things?" she asked. What was her brother up to this time? When he'd first hired Larry last year, it was to shadow Willow Traynor without her knowledge—for her own protection, of course, but she hadn't been happy about it. It had taken some hard convincing for Willow to trust Graham Vaughn again.

"Is the boss around?" Larry asked. "He needs to hear this, too."

Any other time, Ginger would have rolled her eyes at the man's standard reference to her brother, but something in his voice alerted her. "Larry," she said, "what's going on? Just tell me, okay? Graham's already asleep. I was getting ready to turn in, myself. We've got a long day ahead of us tomorrow."

"Hawaii, right?"

She paused. How did he know about that? "That's right. Please don't tell me Graham's contacted you about something and hasn't told us."

"Not yet he hasn't. That's what I called about. I saw the wedding announcement in the paper, and I made a few inquiries. If I could find out so easily, I'm afraid somebody else could've seen it, too."

"Someone like who?"

"Sandi Jameson's killer."

Ginger frowned, confused. "So? That man's in prison. Why should it matter?"

There was silence, and Ginger felt a knot of tension tighten in her stomach. "Larry? Please tell me that monster *is* in prison."

A tired sigh. "I didn't figure you'd get a call from the police in Kansas. State line and all that. Nobody wants to step on anyone else's toes. But I'd've thought somebody'd at least give you guys the heads-up."

"Are you trying to tell me Rick Fenrow has been let out of prison?"

"Nobody *let* him out, that's for sure. He *broke* out."

The fingers of Ginger's left hand tingled. She

realized her grip on the receiver might crack the hard plastic, and she shifted to the other hand.

"Ginger? You there?"

This couldn't be happening. "When?"

"Two days ago. He was in the infirmary—"

"Why did they allow a convicted killer to work in the infirmary? Are they crazy?" And why *hadn't* someone called them sooner? This was unconscionable.

"I didn't say he was working there, I said he was there." Larry sounded tense, himself. "He purportedly injured his leg. From there he coaxed a medical supply delivery lady to slip him out underneath her truck."

"How did he convince her to do that?"

"What can I say? Bad boys do seem to have their charm for some women. I've seen it happen too many times. She's been arrested."

"Shouldn't someone have checked the truck before they allowed it to leave the prison grounds?"

"Yep. The guard who neglected that part of his job has been fired."

Somehow, that failed to comfort Ginger. "But they haven't found Fenrow?" The tingle of alarm spread over her shoulders and down her back.

"Not a clue where he went," Larry said gently. "Look, the boss is going to need to know about this, that crazy loon could be headed toward Hideaway with revenge on his mind."

Ginger shot a sudden glance out into the darkness beyond the bay window and the deck. "Let me talk to Graham. I'll have him call you back."

"You do that. I have a feeling I'm going to need to pack for a trip to Hawaii for some protective surveillance."

Ginger hung up. Had it been anyone else, she'd be tempted to suspect he was making it all up to con them into taking him with them to Hawaii. Larry Bager had the chutzpah to pull it off, too, but he wasn't the type. She knew for a fact he didn't like flying, and he didn't like water.

She decided to check into Rick Fenrow's whereabouts before waking Graham, but she had an awful tightening in her gut that told her Larry Bager knew exactly what he was talking about. Last year's horror was paying another visit.

TWO

Lucy inched along the broad hallway as Aunt Ginger talked to somebody on the telephone, then Lucy crouched behind the coats on the hall stand when Aunt Ginger hung up and hurried in Lucy's direction.

Aunt Ginger wouldn't be mad at Lucy for being up, because she knew Lucy often couldn't sleep. But Lucy realized from the tone of Aunt Ginger's voice that something was going on. She knew from past experience that no one would tell her what it was.

Nobody ever told Lucy anything around here. They thought they were protecting her, when really they were killing her. Curiosity was an awful thing to die from.

Aunt Ginger knocked on Graham's door.

There was no answer. Aunt Ginger always joked about how easy Graham could wake up if he received an emergency call from a patient, but try to wake him up any other time, and it was like waking the dead.

Lucy thought of her dream about Mama. It would be horrible to wake the dead. But Graham wasn't anything like Mama. And he was really alive.

Lucy'd never had a father before. She didn't know

what she was going to call Graham after the adoption was final. "Daddy" sounded too childish, but Aunt Ginger reminded her that she *was* a child, and that "Daddy" was a good name for a real father who loved his little girls.

If Graham wanted her to call him Daddy, that was what she'd do. It was what Brittany already called him, but Lucy had decided she was going to do this right. When Graham and Willow were married, when they came back and signed the adoption papers, then they'd all be a family, and then Lucy would call Graham and Willow what they should be called.

Sure, Lucy already called Aunt Ginger "Aunt." And she called Willow's brother, Preston, "Uncle." But a mother and father were different from other relatives.

Graham finally muttered something from his bedroom that Lucy didn't quite hear, and Aunt Ginger opened the door and stuck her head through. "Graham, something's come up. You need to call your pee eye."

Lucy wrinkled her nose. *Eeww!*

Graham muttered something she couldn't hear.

Aunt Ginger went inside, and Lucy crept closer to the door. She hadn't been able to hear what the call was about earlier, but she could tell Aunt Ginger was upset. Her words were clipped, her voice higher and her speech faster than usual.

"Fenrow's out of prison," she said. "He broke out."

"What do you mean, broke out?" Graham nearly shouted.

"Shhh! You'll wake the girls."

"Did Larry say how it happened? Are you sure this

isn't some practical New Year's Eve joke? He's not drunk, is he?"

"He didn't sound like it. He told me someone sneaked the man past the guards. He's thinking about joining us in Hawaii for protective surveillance."

"How could the guards have allowed Fenrow to slip past them?" Graham asked. "What could they have been thinking? Rick Fenrow, of all people!"

Lucy heard the name clearly. She knew it well. Even though no one would tell her exactly how Mama was killed, Lucy knew, because she'd heard them talking. That man, that Rick Fenrow, was in jail because he killed Mama and tried to kill Willow.

Leaning her forehead against the smooth wood of the hallway wall, Lucy thought she was going to throw up. They were talking about a murderer! And he was out of prison?

"I told Larry you would probably call him back," Aunt Ginger said.

Graham sighed, and there was a long silence. "Larry's presence in Hawaii will put a damper on the whole celebration."

"Isn't it better than the alternative?" Aunt Ginger asked.

"We don't need a reminder about what happened last year. Fenrow surely can't follow us to Hawaii."

"And yet, we don't need to take chances with our lives," Aunt Ginger said. "You know how vindictive Fenrow can be. The man's crazy, Graham, and Larry knew we were going to Hawaii tomorrow, though no one told him. If Larry can find out, so can Fenrow."

Lucy swallowed hard. Last year, Rick Fenrow had set

fire to the cabin where Willow was staying with her brother, Preston. Rick Fenrow was evil and wicked, and evil people always wanted to hurt and kill.

"He killed Sandi Jameson to keep her from talking to Willow," Aunt Ginger said. "You know what he's capable of. We have to think of the children. And Willow. They need protection. We all do."

"Larry wasn't able to protect Sandi last year." Graham's voice sounded louder and closer. He'd gotten out of bed.

"You didn't hire him to protect her," Aunt Ginger said. "You hired him to protect Willow."

"He didn't even do a good job of that."

"She's alive, isn't she?" Aunt Ginger said. "Maybe he would have had more luck if Willow had cooperated and told him about the situation before she went barging into it."

Lucy scowled at this criticism against her soon-to-be new mother.

"He knows what to expect now," Aunt Ginger said. "So do the rest of us."

"Fenrow's always been a loose cannon," Graham grumbled. "What makes you think we can predict his actions any more this year than we did last year?"

"Maybe this is one of those times we need to have some faith," Aunt Ginger said. "We all believe you and Willow and the girls were meant to become a family. If that was God's intent, then it will happen. So maybe you need to have some faith that He will be your protector. However, we can take some steps to protect ourselves."

While Aunt Ginger kept preaching to Graham—

that's what Mama would have called it—Lucy tiptoed
back to her bedroom and slipped through the doorway.

A soft, trembling whisper from the darkness reached
her. "Sissy?"

Lucy gasped, nearly wetting her pants. Brittany stood
like a ghost just inside the door, clutching Chuckles by
an ear, sucking the fingers of her other hand.

"What are you doing up?" Lucy snapped at her.

Brittany took the fingers out of her mouth. "You left!
I s-scared! I woke up and…and…you—"

"Okay. It's okay now." Lucy put an arm around
Brittany's shoulders, feeling bad for snapping. Brittany
had outgrown baby talk most of the time, except when
she was scared, then she forgot. Sometimes she still
sucked her fingers.

"Be quiet and get back to bed." Lucy took Brittany
by the shoulders and nudged her in the direction of
her own bed.

"Can I…can I sleep with you some more?"

"Not if you're going to keep getting up and scaring
me like this."

"But you left!"

"I'm back now, okay?"

"I heard Aunt Ginger and Daddy talking—"

"They're planning our trip. And we're missing out on
sleep. I want to be awake for the trip tomorrow. Now
get into bed and sleep!"

After an hour of staring at the dark ceiling, twisting
her comforter into a tangle, Ginger concluded it was
time for some warm milk and a mild sedative.

Tomorrow…no, make that today, since it was after midnight…New Year's Day, they would be in the air for a total of nine hours, with one layover in St. Louis. She hated going without sleep, because then she got cranky with the girls. She hated cranky. They didn't deserve it.

She got out of bed and pulled on her slippers, then crept into the kitchen in her pajamas. Between hot flashes and an overly heated house, she didn't bother with her housecoat. Wait until Willow hit the age of fifty-three, and see if she allowed Graham to keep these saunalike temperatures in this house.

While the milk heated in the microwave, Ginger swallowed a sleeping pill and rubbed her eyes. Willow and Lucy were the ones with the nightmares in this family, but considering Larry Bager's telephone call, Ginger didn't doubt that she might be in line for some frightening dreams.

She settled in her favorite chair at the kitchen table and took a sip of the milk. A wall of glass separated the kitchen from the deck. At this time of year, the deck furniture was stored in the basement, so she had a clear view of the lake, where the water shimmered with light from the full moon.

After talking with Larry, Graham had decided, as she'd known he would, that they could use a watchful private investigator on their trip. Ginger knew the ex-cop was a good P.I., but how was he going to keep up with a group of people who would be scattered across the whole island of Kauai?

After the wedding, Graham and Willow planned to spend most of the week together, exploring the island, in a world all their own. Preston Black, Willow's brother, was going to help Ginger watch the girls. The planners of this exotic wedding, Helen and Steve Courtney, would also be around to act as escorts and help with whatever was needed. This wedding trip was an extravagant gift from Mrs. Engle, a wealthy lady who Graham and Willow had befriended last year, and who had spared no expense in the arrangements she'd made for their comfort and enjoyment.

The children's days would be filled with swimming, hiking, exploring. Graham and Willow didn't want to spend the whole time separated from the girls, so they planned to have dinner most evenings with Lucy and Brittany.

It looked as if Larry Bager would now be helping Ginger, Preston and the Courtneys babysit.

Ginger had taken a second sip of milk when she thought she heard a tap-rattle somewhere at the other end of the house. Probably the wind.

Still…

She pushed away from the table and crept through the dark, quiet house. Before leaving for the medical mission field in Belarus, Ginger had been afraid of things that went bump in the night. Ten years dealing with every situation imaginable in a foreign country had toughened her. Now, it took more than an unidentified noise in the darkness to frighten her; it took recent notification that a convicted murderer had broken out of prison.

She passed her bedroom door and skirted the bentwood coatrack in the hall when a tiny figure in white suddenly appeared, startling her.

"Brittany?" she whispered. "Honey, what are you doing out of bed?"

The child rubbed her eyes and squeezed poor Chuckles so tightly Ginger feared for his head. "Lucy woke me up and now I can't sleep."

Ginger took Brittany's free hand and led her back along the hallway. "How about sharing some warm milk with me?"

"With honey?"

"Sure." Ginger brushed long strands of Brittany's blond hair behind her shoulders, and looked down into the child's green eyes. This little darling looked so much like her late mother that it sometimes chilled Ginger.

The sisters looked nothing alike. Lucy had dark, soulfully deep eyes that seemed to see beneath the surface of things. Her hair was almost as dark as her eyes, her face solemn in repose, whereas Brittany always had a quick smile. Lucy remained aloof from strangers, and it often seemed to concern her when her little sister made friends easily.

The bond of love between the sisters was strong. Lucy took her role as older sister seriously. For the first few months of the girls' life here in Hideaway, Lucy had refused to let Brittany out of her sight.

Keeping watch over the active five-year-old was quite a responsibility, and, after much pleading, Ginger had convinced Lucy that Brittany would come to no harm here in the tiny village of kind, common people.

"How did Lucy wake you up?" Ginger asked.

"She had another bad dream, and then I got into bed with her so she'd feel safe, but she left me there."

Ginger stopped. "She *left* you?"

"Uh-huh. She went out to the hallway when you and Daddy were arguing."

Ginger winced. "We weren't arguing." What if Lucy had overheard her talking to Graham about Rick Fenrow? "Where is she now?"

Before Brittany could answer, a scream rent the air, followed quickly by another, raising the hairs along the back of Ginger's neck and causing her to stumble and stub her toe on the hall coatrack.

That was Lucy's voice, raised in terror.

Another nightmare?

Ginger turned and ran back down the hallway. Graham's door flew open and he scrambled out, nearly colliding with Ginger. The screams continued.

They reached Lucy's room to find her standing between the beds, staring out the window. Graham grabbed her up into his arms while Ginger turned on the light. Lucy's face was as pale as her nightgown, her dark brown eyes wide with terror, mouth open, long hair falling over her face.

"The man, Graham!" she cried, pointing toward the window. "There was a man! He was out there watching me when I opened my eyes. I saw him. He was watching me! Right in that window!"

Graham put Lucy down and grabbed the flashlight the girls kept on the stand between the beds for when the electricity went off. He rushed to the window and shone the bright beam over the yard around the side of the house, then turned and ran from the room. Within seconds, the outdoor lights flooded the yard and garden, outlining two of the horses in the corral behind the house.

Ginger heard Brittany's cries from the kitchen. Grabbing Lucy's hand, she hurried back to find Graham holding Brittany in his arms as he punched a number on the telephone keypad.

"Shhh, it's okay, honey," he whispered to Brittany. "It's going to be okay. Lucy's been having some bad dreams lately, you know—" His attention switched to the phone. "Greg? This is Graham Vaughn. Could you come out here? We've had some excitement." He explained the situation to the sheriff in two succinct sentences, thanked him and hung up, stooping to place Brittany on her feet.

"There'll be some men here in a couple of minutes. I'm going to go outside and check—"

"No!" Lucy cried. "What if it's that man?" She stared, wide-eyed, at Brittany, pressing her lips together. The terror in her eyes told Ginger what she'd feared.

Indeed, Lucy had heard them earlier tonight. She obviously knew about Rick Fenrow.

"Graham," Ginger said, "why don't you stay inside?" More than likely, Lucy had awakened from another nightmare, and convinced herself it was real because of what she'd overheard. More than likely.

But Ginger didn't want to take chances. And so the four of them stayed together in the kitchen, staring out the windows, the children wide-eyed and trembling, until they heard the sound of a motor a few minutes later.

As they'd expected, the sheriff and his deputy, as well as Taylor Jackson, forest ranger, arrived in three different vehicles—Taylor's vehicle being a boat.

This sprawling log home provided them with the

best of both worlds. They lived in the country, with all the privacy they could want. They were only a quarter of a mile from downtown Hideaway by way of the shoreline, and one mile by road. Many Hideaway residents used water transportation.

The men searched the entire property. By the time they were finished, Dane Gideon, mayor of Hideaway and director of the boys' ranch across the lake, had come over. With him were his household help, Richard Cook, and college student, Blaze Farmer, who, Ginger knew, Lucy adored. If anyone could put Lucy at ease about tonight, it would be Blaze.

All the men went over the property once again for good measure, then rejoined the family in the great room, accepting the cups of hot chocolate the girls had helped Ginger prepare.

No one was found, but Ginger couldn't help feeling that perhaps someone just didn't *want* to be found.

THREE

Ray Clyde sat reading the *Springfield Daily News* with his back to the window that looked out over the parking lot of the Springfield-Branson Airport. He'd received an early morning summons to Columbia Regional Hospital for one of his young patients. After finishing there, he'd decided just to drive on down to Springfield rather than go back to bed. He'd have had to get up early to make the three-hour drive, anyway.

It was never easy to get back to sleep after dealing with a child in pain, though after twenty years, he should be impervious to the cries of mother and child, the fear and panic. He wasn't. He had decided when he first began his career that if he ever ceased to have compassion for his patients, he would retire.

He'd be working well into his seventies at this rate.

He glanced over the top of his paper as two familiar figures entered the concourse and walked toward the Delta self-check-in terminals. He smiled at the sight of Willow Traynor and her brother, Preston Black.

Willow glowed with the radiance of a woman in love. Tall and slender, with short, dark hair, she emanated self-sufficiency. This was something about which her fiancé, Graham Vaughn, occasionally complained—though always with good grace.

Neither Willow nor Preston noticed Ray, and he was glad. It meant others also might not notice him. Graham had even suggested that Ray not attempt to board until the last minute. Ray understood perfectly why his friend felt a late arrival was necessary, but he still chafed at the thought of subterfuge.

After another five minutes, the glass doors slid open again and two little girls burst into the concourse. Ray knew from photos that these children were Lucy and Brittany Jameson. They would be adopted by Graham and Willow next week, as soon as they returned from Hawaii.

"Mommy!" Brittany called, racing forward, arms outstretched.

Willow turned, a smile of delight spreading across the slightly angular features of her face. The smile transformed her somewhat solemn expression into a thing of beauty.

She and her brother, Preston, both stepped out of line and knelt to embrace the children.

Brittany, the five-year-old, looked small for her age, though Ray knew she was nearly six. It was easy to tell that she was the charmer. With long, pale hair and a wide grin, she looked much like the photos of her mother, who had been killed last year.

Lucy, in contrast, appeared older than eight and a half, not because of her size, but because her demeanor was so watchful and serious. She resembled Willow, with her dark brown hair and reserved expression, especially when she smiled, which she suddenly did at Willow, whom she obviously adored.

Preston leaned close to Lucy and asked her something. Ray couldn't hear what he said, but Lucy placed her hands on her hips and gave him a disapproving look. "It's not an airplane, Uncle Preston, it's a jet."

Preston chuckled. He, too, looked most like Willow when he smiled. It was obvious he doted on the children.

"That's right, my dear, you set 'em straight" came a painfully familiar voice from behind the girls.

Ray looked up to see Ginger Carpenter walking through the doorway beside Graham Vaughn, her brother. Ray's breath caught.

Ginger. A year ago, if anyone had suggested that a rift might form between him and Ginger Carpenter, Ray would have thought it was impossible. His most precious memories of their time together and their growing friendship were of her smile, her laughter, her tender compassion.

Of course, many of those same memories also included the powerful and painful attraction he had felt for her since their first meeting. By all indications, the attraction had never been reciprocated, and he hoped his rare loss of emotional control had remained undetected by his colleagues—and especially by Ginger.

He expected her to turn at any second and spot him. Fireworks would then commence.

The reason Graham preferred that the conflagration take place onboard rather than in the concourse was obvious. Graham wanted his sister to attend his wedding. If she saw Ray while she could still escape, she might do so. Graham had warned Ray that his characteristically kindhearted, forgiving sister had not forgiven Ray for their conflict last year.

Ray intended for that to change on this trip.

He continued to hold the paper, but over the top edge he watched Ginger. He had always enjoyed her sunny smile, her quick laughter, the glow of health across her fair, freckled face. This morning her golden-red hair was mingled with new silver that he hadn't noticed a year ago. The effect was one of antiqued copper—very becoming on her. She didn't appear well rested, however.

A strange man with dark brown hair and a black leather jacket suddenly joined the group. Lucy grabbed her sister's arm and stepped in front of her protectively.

Ray watched the man's face.

"Ow!" Brittany wriggled from Lucy's grip. "Stop it, sissy, you're hurting me."

Lucy released her, but continued to stare at the man. As Preston and Willow had done, this man squatted in front of the girls, looking them in the eyes. "Hi. I'm Larry Bager."

The man's eyes were dark brown, and his well-developed muscles beneath the jacket were obvious. He had a short beard that looked unshaved rather than intentionally grown.

"I'm Lucy Jameson," the older sister told the man. "This is my sister, Brittany."

He nodded. "I know."

Lucy leaned closer to him and said something Ray

couldn't hear. Larry's gaze flicked up to Ginger, then back at Lucy. "That's right, I'm like a bodyguard."

Lucy nodded, apparently satisfied. "Is that like a bouncer? I went to work with Mama sometimes, and she introduced me to the bouncer at the bar where she worked."

Again, Larry nodded. "I'm the man to come to if you get scared of anything, okay?"

"Okay."

Larry straightened and looked around. "Hey, boss," he said to Graham, "where're those trip escorts we're supposed to have flying with us?"

"I just got a call from Helen Courtney," Graham said. "She told me they had some car trouble and they're running late, but they'll be on the flight with us."

Larry was close enough to Ray when he drew Graham aside that Ray could hear them. "You check 'em out? Are they legit?"

"One of my renters, Mrs. Engle, set us up with them. They've been on board with this plan for several weeks, coordinating our requests."

Larry glanced in Ray's direction and his eyes narrowed, as if some inner radar ignited his suspicion. "Can't be too careful."

Lucy grabbed her sister's hand. "Brittany, you've got to stay with us, okay?" Lucy said. "No wandering off, and you can't talk to strangers. I mean it."

"Okay." Brittany turned and smiled up at Larry Bager, even though she'd just met him. "My teacher says airplanes are as safe as riding a school bus."

Lucy nudged Brittany. "School bus? Not even close. You aren't with a bunch of kids on this flight. These are grown-ups, and you know what Mama always said about talking to strangers, especially grown-ups."

Aunt Ginger gave Lucy one of her raised-eyebrow looks over her shoulder. "Stop with the fear tactics, my dear. It'll only make things worse." She gave a sharp nod.

Lucy knew what the nod meant. It meant: *Especially after scaring Brittany to death last night.*

But that hadn't been a dream standing in the window, and Lucy knew it, no matter how much Aunt Ginger tried to convince her everything was okay.

Lucy had seen Rick Fenrow. She knew the difference between a dream and a real man. She could close her eyes and see that face. Shaggy black hair, shaggy black eyebrows that looked like caterpillars. White face.

Brittany probably didn't even remember how scared everybody had been last night. Those kinds of things never bothered her much. Why should they? Lucy was always there to make sure nobody hurt her. Brittany didn't know everything about Mama's killer.

Last night, even with Blaze Farmer and Dane Gideon standing guard at opposite ends of the house until morning, Lucy hadn't been able to sleep.

Why couldn't Blaze come with them to Hawaii? Blaze was strong and kind, and he didn't think he was too good to talk to little girls.

But Blaze had already agreed to take care of the farm for Graham while they were gone, so he couldn't go with them.

Lucy kept a lookout for the man she'd seen last night.

Once in the jet, settled in her seat by the window, she studied everyone who entered.

Aunt Ginger sat in the seat between Lucy and Brittany. Uncle Preston sat directly across the aisle from them, with Willow and Graham in front of him.

Once, Lucy had asked if Aunt Ginger and Uncle Preston were boyfriend and girlfriend. Aunt Ginger had laughed, saying that, biologically, she was old enough to be Uncle Preston's mother.

Lucy didn't know what biologically meant, but Uncle Preston had a girlfriend now. Her name was Sheila, and she was nice.

Aunt Ginger had said more than once that she wasn't a romantic type. She said she knew better than to make that mistake again. Graham laughed at her, but she talked as if she meant it. She said, "Graham Vaughn, don't you go trying to set me up with any of those friends of yours. I'm out of commission, and I like it that way."

Two old people sat down next to Uncle Preston, introducing themselves as Helen and Steve Courtney, the travel coordinators and escorts. The woman immediately started talking to Brittany, who chattered away, as if they were old friends or something. The dummy! If Rick Fenrow himself ever tried to take Brittany's hand and lead her away, she would probably go with him, chattering to him until he cut her throat.

Lucy and Larry Bager would have their hands full with Brittany.

Helen and Steve Courtney were even older than Aunt Ginger, who liked to brag that she "needed to be accorded respect because of her advanced age of fifty-three." Lucy didn't know what accorded meant, and she griped at Aunt Ginger for using big words without explaining them.

Helen Courtney had a camera, and she started taking pictures of everything and everybody, especially Graham and Willow, Lucy and Brittany, right there on the jet.

The Courtneys made Lucy nervous. Why did Helen Courtney have to take so many pictures?

"Honey, I'm going to be taking all the pictures you'll ever want on this trip," she explained, patting Willow's hand. "I'll even catch some shots you'll want to erase, but not many! I know my stuff. I'm making memories for a lifetime, you know."

Lucy studied the woman. She seemed to smile all the time. She had a lot of wrinkles around her eyes and mouth, and she wore more makeup than Aunt Ginger or Willow ever did.

"I love your hair," Aunt Ginger told Helen. "It's the perfect shade for you."

Helen laughed. "Oopsie! You caught me there." She patted her hair as if it might be out of place. "Fresh from the bottle."

Lucy stared at the woman's hair. Must be a big bottle. Was she bald under there?

Helen's husband, Steve, had gray hair and lots of wrinkles around his eyes, too. He didn't smile as much as Helen. Lucy was relieved that he didn't look anything like the man at the window last night.

Larry Bager sat in the seat behind Helen. He didn't

say much, but he stared at every person who got on the airplane.

Brittany suddenly looked up from her unzipped backpack, eyes wide, mouth open with horror. "Oh no! Aunt Ginger, I forgot to pack Chuckles! You told me to be sure to pack him and I forgot! Did you pack him? You did, didn't you Aunt Ginger? Huh?"

Ginger had realized last night that this wasn't going to be an easy trip. With the lack of sleep and the fright the girls—and she and Graham—had endured, her mind hadn't been as sharp as she'd have liked. But this? It was inexcusable.

"Oh, honey, I'm so sorry, but—"

"No!" Brittany wailed. "We can't go without Chuckles! We've got to go back and get him, we've *got* to!"

It seemed the eye of every person in the aisles around them turned to see what Ginger was going to do about the panicky child. Some passengers were amused, some irritated.

Brittany started to cry.

Lucy tapped Ginger on the arm. "Aunt Ginger." She held up her backpack, and slowly unzipped the largest compartment.

Two fuzzy golden ears popped up, and Lucy pulled the teddy bear out.

Brittany squealed with delight. Helen Courtney clapped, and several people around them laughed.

Ginger threw her arms around her little heroine and kissed her on the forehead. "Sweetheart, you're the best big sister in the world." She leaned back and enjoyed the glow of satisfaction she saw in Lucy's dark eyes. "I'm so proud of you."

A smile actually spread across Lucy's face. Ginger wished she could see that smile more often. This quiet little girl had been through so much in the past nine months. The ordeal of her mother's murder, living with strangers, and now being afraid of her mother's killer, had matured her far beyond her years. Ginger grieved that tragic loss of innocence.

At least the incident with Chuckles had distracted Lucy from her morbid search for Rick Fenrow—for the moment. That was Larry's job, and from the looks of it, he would do it well.

Brittany held her teddy bear up for Helen's inspection. "His name is Chuckles, because he used to laugh when I squeezed his paw."

Helen reached out and squeezed the bear's paw. Nothing happened.

"He doesn't laugh anymore," Brittany explained. "Lucy says he's grieving because Mama died."

"I'm sure he is." Helen's voice caught, and her face suddenly lined with sorrow.

Brittany nodded. "He stopped laughing the day Mama died."

Ginger glanced at Larry, then at the people coming on board. She, too, felt a compelling need to protect these children, at any cost.

Her gaze traveled down the queue, then stopped at a familiar face. She caught her breath as she studied the big man with black hair, dark blue eyes, and shoulders as broad as a linebacker's.

"No," she whispered. Ray Clyde.

Of all people, what was her worst enemy on earth doing on this flight?

Ray grimaced when a teenager stepped backward onto his foot, but the pain wasn't as sharp as the look in Ginger Carpenter's eyes when she caught sight of him from her seat near the middle of the main cabin.

He hadn't expected anything else. And how could he blame her? If he was in her position, he'd probably feel the same way.

He'd hoped for a meeting under better circumstances, however. Graham had warned him not to try to contact her in any way.

How had it come to this?

An elderly lady turned in the aisle to ask if someone could place her suitcase in the overhead compartment. Glad for the distraction, Ray hurried to her aid. This day had suddenly grown a lot more interesting…and a lot more volatile.

FOUR

Ginger steadied herself, sure she'd felt the jet shift, though the door remained open and people continued to enter.

She blinked and tried to refocus, but still he was there. No mistake about it. It was Dr. Ray Clyde. As usual, he stood taller than every other man by at least a couple of inches. His size, his voice, his rugged-but-attractive face and demeanor all drew attention to his commanding presence.

He'd been her director when she was on the mission field in Belarus. At one time, she'd believed they had a special relationship—not romantic, perhaps, but she'd thought they were the best of friends. He seemed to be such a caring man, and at one time she'd thought he'd cared deeply about her—at least as a friend.

Then came the betrayal.

The line of passengers entering the jet came to a standstill while an elderly woman asked for help placing her luggage in an overhead compartment. Ray helped her, of course. Ray was always jumping to someone's aid. Everyone's but Ginger's.

After easily lifting the piece of luggage for the lady, he accepted her thanks with a silent nod, then looked up and caught Ginger's gaze. Ginger could not look away. All the pain and fury of his betrayal surfaced, and her hands clenched at her sides.

She broke the connection at last, and unbuckled her seat belt. She stood and turned to glare at Graham across the aisle.

As if he'd been waiting for her to react, he looked up at her, then winced at the look on her face. Willow, seated beside him, saw her, too, and her blue-gray eyes filled with compassion—but not surprise.

Both of them had known Ray would be here.

Ginger felt doubly betrayed. Whatever was going on, Willow was obviously as involved as Graham.

Ginger could say nothing in this crowd, in front of the girls, with several strangers within earshot. She couldn't protest, couldn't threaten to take the girls and deplane, as much as the idea tempted her at this moment. But her anger continued to grow. How dare they?

Graham sighed, got up, and stepped across the aisle, leaning close to Ginger's ear. "I gather there's a problem."

"How insightful of you," she hissed through gritted teeth. "Don't you try to tell me Ray Clyde's presence on this jet is coincidence."

"I wouldn't dare."

"What's he doing here?"

There was a hesitation, then Graham said softly, "He's going with us to Hawaii."

Though she'd already guessed what her brother would say, she caught her breath sharply. Betrayal, indeed. "Did you tell him to wait and board at the last moment so I couldn't change my mind about going?"

Graham winced again. "I knew the timing would be tight, since he had to drive down from Columbia after a meeting this morning."

"I'm sure you counted on it." A wave of heat spread over her face and neck, and for once, it wasn't a hot flash. How *dare* he?

"Sorry, Ginger," he said softly. "I wanted to discuss it with you, but I knew you would find some reason to back out if you discovered he was coming."

"You've got that right." She looked down at Brittany, who sat happily playing with her bear, and then glanced around at Lucy, who was watching her with curiosity.

She must not lose her temper further. Graham obviously had used the seating arrangements for his purpose, as well.

Ginger was going to have to torture her brother at a later date.

"Ray has been a good friend of mine for many years." Graham kept his voice low. "I couldn't exclude him from this wedding. It's too important. He was there for me when I needed a friend after the divorce."

Ginger gritted her teeth. "I was there for you, too. Just because I was halfway around the world—"

"I know you were there in spirit. Ray let me stay at his place until I could find my own. Ray gave me references when I needed a new job. He's been supportive from the—"

"Please stop." Ginger closed her eyes. It hurt to hear

her beloved brother singing the praises of a manipulative, hard hearted…

"He isn't the jerk you believe him to be," Graham said.

For Ginger, two nightmares were coming true in a few short hours. Rick Fenrow was out of prison, and her backstabbing ex-director was undermining her relationship with her brother. How could Graham do this to her?

"So he's in the wedding party," she said.

Graham nodded.

"And what part does he play?"

Graham looked over his shoulder at Willow, then back at Ginger. "He's going to be best man."

Ginger caught her breath. Of course. She was going to be matron of honor, and Ray would be best man. "What a wonderful way to begin a marriage, when the main witnesses to the wedding hate each other."

"That isn't true, Ginger. Ray holds no animosity toward you at all. In fact, he's eager to make amends."

"I thought Preston was going to be best man," she said. After all, Willow's brother *should* hold that place of honor.

"I had initially asked Ray to do the honors, and then there was a glitch, and he thought he was going to have to fly to Africa. That was when I asked Preston. The situation changed, and Ray was able to join us, after all. I think Preston was glad to be relieved of any responsibility."

"You'd better find yourself another matron of honor, then, Graham."

"Please, sis, don't be this way."

Ginger turned to look at Ray once more. He was advancing slowly down the aisle, waiting patiently as people in front of him took their time stowing their carry-on luggage.

He caught her gaze again, his dark blue eyes probing—perhaps to gauge the force of her reaction? How could he not know what it would be? Did he expect her to welcome him with open arms?

"Ginger," Willow called, patting the seat beside her. "Come sit with me a minute. We need to talk."

Ginger hesitated. She didn't want to talk, she wanted to scream. If it were anyone but Willow...

She crossed the aisle and sat in the seat Graham had vacated. "Don't you think this is an awkward time to be explaining things? Am I a child who has to be manipulated?"

Willow spread her hands. "Well, in this instance—"

"Don't *you* start with me, too. Graham is bad enough, but I know he's a control freak. I'd have thought better of you."

"Give it some time, okay?" Willow said. "Preston's been willing to stand in as best man for Graham, but he knew Graham had asked Ray. Believe me, I know my brother. Preston wasn't disappointed to be given the chance to step down."

"No one thought about giving *me* the chance to step down."

"I wanted you to be there for me."

Ginger didn't want to argue, especially with Willow. Graham and Willow deserved their wedding trip to go smoothly. After all the suffering they had gone through in the past years, Willow and Graham needed something to go right.

But this…this was far from acceptable.

"This was what you and Graham and Preston were talking about on Christmas Day when I walked into the room and everyone fell silent," Ginger said.

"Sorry. I really hated keeping it from you."

"Then you shouldn't have."

"That remains to be seen."

Again, irritation prickled along Ginger's skin. "You know, my brother hasn't changed as much as he wants to believe. Unfortunately, I think his tactics are rubbing off on you. Now both of you are controlling the lives of others."

"Then I guess that's a trait that runs in the family," Willow said drily. "I seem to remember a lady who refused to take no for an answer when I needed a place to stay after the cabin burned last spring. I was a complete stranger to you, and you took me in."

"Don't change the subject," Ginger said. "Don't you think a fifty-three-year-old woman should be given the option to choose with whom she spends her time?"

Willow finally had the grace to look abashed. "Of course."

"Except when it comes to me, is that right?" Ginger asked.

"I think we all tend to take extra liberties when it comes to close family members, who we know will have to forgive us, because they have such a forgiving nature."

"Don't patronize me," Ginger warned. "It won't work. My conflict with Ray Clyde is my business and no one else's."

"Then you'll be happy to keep it to yourself until after the wedding, right?" Willow's tone grew slightly sharper.

A familiar, masculine scent of spice alerted Ginger that Ray had reached them. She looked up at him looking down at her.

"Hello, Ginger," he said quietly.

She nodded, startled at the look of vulnerability in those eyes.

Graham rose from Ginger's seat across the aisle and greeted Ray, pumping his hand. They were best friends reuniting after a long time apart. It stung. It did more than sting, it stabbed at her.

Her brother had no idea what kind of game he was playing this time, but he wasn't going to win. If he had some crazy notion of mediating a peace, he was in for a disappointing trip.

FIVE

Ray Clyde had always been able to read Ginger Carpenter's thoughts in her face. It wasn't a difficult accomplishment, nor was it even necessary most of the time. Ginger rarely minced words, and she seldom concealed her emotions. She said what she thought.

Today, Ray was glad he wasn't sitting near her for the first leg of the flight. Judging by the daggers she shot at him with her glare, he might be bleeding profusely by the time they reached Lambert International in St. Louis.

Quiet, watchful Lucy tapped Ginger on the arm.

The daggers left Ginger's eyes, and that same gaze filled with gentleness and love as she listened to the child.

Ray was lost once again. He had known it would happen. He'd been half in love with the talkative and strong-willed woman since their first meeting. The more he'd come to know her, the more he'd admired her vibrant spirit and caring heart.

But it was also her caring heart that had placed a wedge between them later, when he was forced to make a difficult decision. Ginger had always been passionate about what she believed in—a trait that he found extremely attractive, even though it created complications from time to time.

Ray and Ginger had become good friends during her time in Belarus. They had even shared a few friendly meals together when she was home on furlough, and Ray had enjoyed it much more than was comfortable—he'd always wanted more time with her. He'd known, however, that the clinic she directed in Minsk was the top priority in her life. He'd always honored that priority and admired her dedication to it.

Ray's place was not in Belarus, but in Columbia, Missouri. Located in the center of the state and the center of the United States, Columbia enabled him to be on a flight anywhere in the country or the world in a short period. This way he could keep his finger on the pulse of GlobeMed.

His personal mission was located right there in Columbia. Young doctors came straight out of med school and residencies in that university town, hungry for work and experience, and idealistic about the future. Ray's goal was to reach as many of them as possible before their idealism gave way to materialism. His desire was to show as many young doctors as he could the joys of true service.

Yearlong mission trips in places of greatest need—mostly third world countries torn by war and famine—gave these doctors not only valuable experience working with the sickest of patients, but a better grasp of the needs of the larger world that didn't revolve around a life of ease and luxuries.

If only those young grads would realize what was

truly important in life. It was not the size of their homes, or the number of cars, or bank balances they could acquire. Their true calling was to touch and heal the hurting, no matter the financial reward.

Sometimes, in his efforts to reach the most people, Ray knew he failed others. It broke his heart that Ginger thought she had been a casualty of that mission.

After the jet took off and the seat belt light went off, Graham came down the aisle and slid into the empty seat across from Ray.

"That went over well, I think," Graham said drily.

"Could've been worse," Ray agreed.

Graham chuckled. "I consider it an achievement that she didn't grab the girls and leave."

"Definitely encouraging. Tell me something, Graham. Did you ask me to be your best man for the sole purpose of helping me work out the knots between your sister and myself?"

"I asked you to be my best man years ago, remember? After my divorce, when I was staying with you. I told you if I ever got married again, you would be my best man, and you said I would be yours. So now you need to give me a chance to return the favor."

Ray gave him a look. "That's what I thought."

"Ginger's frustrated, Ray. I've tried to keep her busy at my clinic, and she's been working some hours at the Hideaway Hospital when the girls are in school. But I know Ginger. She's restless. She's never come to terms with what happened last year. I'd like to see her do that."

"I thought you had her working with you at your free clinic."

Graham sighed and sat back, shaking his head at the flight attendant with the beverage cart. "That isn't the kind of challenge she needs. It isn't as satisfying as we had first hoped. There are so many who aren't willing to pay their own way, when they are perfectly capable of doing so. Ginger's spent more time screening patients for genuine need than she's spent in the treatment room."

"I would imagine she's good at it. She's always had a knack for reading a person's thoughts. Uncanny." Uncomfortable, too.

"Last week she had to inform a businesswoman who makes more than a hundred fifty thou a year that she wasn't eligible for a free elective surgery," Graham said.

"Hasn't the woman ever heard of insurance?"

"Her complaint was it costs too much. Ginger's tired of it. Her most fulfilling task lately has been caring for Lucy and Brittany, and this trip represents the end of that role. Willow's ecstatic about the adoption. Ginger, on the other hand, has been despondent for days."

"What about you?" Ray asked, studying Graham's pensive expression. "You're not adopting the girls just to please Willow, are you?"

"No. I honestly can't imagine life without those two little girls in it now. Their primary residence has been with Ginger and me, and I find myself resenting the time I have to spend at work because I can't spend it with the people I love, both Willow and the children."

Ray smiled at his friend. "I couldn't be happier for you, Graham. It's been a long time coming."

Graham nodded. "The time was right, as it never had been before."

Ray and Graham had met fourteen years ago, when Graham was in surgical residency. Even then, Ray had sought opportunities to help recruit the brightest and best for GlobeMed. To his disappointment, Graham was snatched by one of the most sought-after surgical practice groups in Springfield, Missouri, as soon as he was out of residency.

Because of their continued friendship, however, Ray knew Graham's most cherished desire was to have a family. His first wife had chosen not to have children. When she divorced him, it had hit him hard, and he had given up on his dream.

Willow Traynor was an answer to Ray's prayers for his friend. The widow of a murdered cop, she had lost their baby when her husband's murderer ran her down with a car nearly three years ago. Last year, that vicious murderer had hunted her down in Branson and tried, again, to destroy her life, and the lives of those around her.

Some might say Lucy and Brittany's mother had been collateral damage, because she had interfered with Willow's stalker—had even tried to warn Willow about the danger while in a drugged stupor. That drugged stupor had cost the poor woman her life.

Since last April, Willow had blossomed with the friendship of Graham and Ginger, and the adoration of those two little girls. From what Ray had heard about the children, their lives were far better now than when they were with their confused and drug-addicted mother. But try telling that to Lucy and Brittany. Graham had told Ray last week that Lucy still had nightmares about her mother's death.

"After this week," Graham said, "Ginger will be lost without the girls."

"That's a bad place for Ginger to be." Ray had never known anyone with such a need to care for someone.

He'd never known someone who drew him so.

"I'm not really trying to matchmake," Graham said. "Though I'm sure that's what Ginger thinks I'm doing."

Ray shot a wicked grin at Graham. "Ginger knows her brother pretty well, I think."

Graham chuckled. "Honestly, matchmaking's Willow's territory."

"And you think she might have something like that in mind?"

"It's possible."

Ray shook his head. "You've never been a good liar. You're in this up to your eyeballs, I can tell."

"I don't like to see my sister so miserable."

"In case you hadn't noticed, she appears to be pretty miserable now that I've boarded."

"A good heart-to-heart could unravel a few tangles, I think," Graham said.

"Please don't tell me you're going to try to convince me to send her back to Minsk."

"Not at all," Graham said quickly. "I want her stateside. That heart trouble she had last year spooked me, even though it turned out to be a harmless arrhythmia. What I want is to see her forgive you."

"I'd like that, too." Ray sighed, frowning at the puzzle that had confused him since his conflict with Ginger last March. "I've never known her to hold a grudge. She's changed her guiding principle at this stage in her life—and the grudge is with me. It isn't a comfortable place to be."

"She's been hurt deeply. I'd like to see you two work out whatever complications have developed between you."

Ray nodded. Ginger Carpenter would be a definite complication on this trip. "I'll see what I can do, but don't get your hopes up."

Ginger glanced over her shoulder and saw Ray and Graham with their heads together. As she continued to watch suspiciously, Ray glanced up and caught her gaze.

She held it. He needed to understand that she wasn't going to just forget the past as if it hadn't happened. She'd love to be able to do just that, but it would be dishonest. She'd tried to forgive, just as the Bible said to do. She'd even heard the reminder in church yesterday—forgive your enemy.

Forgive. The minister had said nothing about forgetting, and that was good, because she thought that was a stupid idea. If someone stabs you in the back, are you smart to forget, and give them the chance to do it again?

She wasn't that kind of fool. She'd done a lot of stupid things in her life, but she'd learned from her mistakes, especially the one she'd made with Ray Clyde.

Ray's expression told her that he and her brother were discussing her blatant, rude response to Ray's presence. Fine. Let 'em talk.

The plane landed, they de-boarded, and Ginger took Brittany's hand to keep her close. The child had a tendency to wander away.

Lucy suddenly gasped and dragged Ginger to a stop.

"It's him, Aunt Ginger. It looks just like him!" Pointing at a slender, dark-haired man in the concourse, Lucy shook with fear.

SIX

Ginger had grown so attuned to Lucy and Brittany that she had known before Lucy even stopped her that she was suddenly in a panic. Her eyes, glistening with fear, were so wide, her expression so vulnerable that it broke Ginger's heart.

Ginger followed Lucy's line of vision, and indeed, saw a teenager who looked a lot like Rick Fenrow. He had thick, black hair, a pale, almost gaunt face, and eyebrows that looked like untamable caterpillars.

"No, honey. It's okay," she said, squatting to face Lucy, to hold her gaze and assure her she was safe. "That young man isn't Rick."

Lucy stared into her eyes, sober, serious, probing, as if attempting to discern if Ginger was merely trying to placate her.

"You've seen Rick Fenrow, Lucy," she said softly. "We both know what he looks like, and if that was him," she said, pointing at the kid, "I'd be calling for the police. You can trust me. Rick is older than this young man by at least ten or fifteen years."

Lucy blinked then and sighed quietly, and Ginger saw some of the tension leave her face. "Okay."

Ginger glanced up to find Ray's gaze on her again, and the expression on his face suggested that he was trying to determine the wisdom of joining her in her efforts to reassure Lucy.

Did he know about the prison break? He looked confused.

"He's a doppelgänger," Ginger said.

Lucy frowned. "Huh?"

Ginger tried not to smile. Whenever Lucy heard a new word, she was distracted for hours trying to pronounce it and understand it. "That means you're looking at someone who seems familiar, but really isn't. That young man over there isn't Rick, because he's a kid. See, those are probably his parents with him." She pointed to a middle-aged couple walking beside the youngster. To Lucy, of course, a teenage boy would look like a grown man.

What concerned Ginger was that Lucy obviously did know what Rick Fenrow looked like. That might be because she remembered him from last year, when he lived in the same apartment complex. It might also be because she'd gotten a good look at him in the window last night.

Ginger didn't want to even think about that.

Oh, Lord, protect us.

Lucy watched the dopoganer—or whatever it was Aunt Ginger called him—hand his ticket to somebody in a uniform, then follow a line of people out of sight. He didn't look at Lucy once.

Maybe that was because he really didn't know her. Or maybe it was because he didn't want her to know he knew her. What if he was pretending? What if he came back and grabbed her or Brittany when no one was looking?

Trying to think like a killer wasn't easy.

She wanted to watch to make sure he didn't come back, but Willow took her by the hand.

"Come on, sweetheart. We've got a short layover, and a lot of walking to do to get to our next gate."

Graham picked up Brittany and carried her on ahead of them. Uncle Preston walked on Lucy's other side, with his hand on her shoulder and his other hand holding his cell phone while he talked to his girl-friend, Sheila.

Uncle Preston was big and strong. Lucy felt safe with him.

She felt safe with Willow, too. Willow was tall and strong and brave.

Last year, the night the fire broke out at Uncle Preston's cabin, Willow had broken into the apartment to rescue Lucy and Brittany because she couldn't get them to answer the door. She had been the first person to discover they were alone at night while Mama worked. That was when she argued with Mama, and then started babysitting them so they wouldn't be alone.

Lucy looked at Willow's arm, and with her fingers she traced the scar Willow had gotten from cutting herself on the window when she broke in to save them. "Does this still hurt sometimes?"

Willow smiled down at her. "Nope. It doesn't even itch now."

Lucy would never tell anybody this, but she loved looking at that scar. Every time she saw it, she remembered that Willow would do anything to protect her and Brittany. And that was even before she was going to adopt them.

"Are Brittany and me in danger?" Lucy asked softly.

Willow's steps slowed and stopped, and she knelt down to look into Lucy's eyes, right there in the middle of that crowded hallway in the airport. Lucy had heard people say she looked as if she could be Willow's daughter, with the same dark eyebrows and hair.

Lucy wanted to look like Willow. She wanted to act like her, too, strong and kind and brave. And she never wanted to do drugs or act crazy, like Mama.

"Honey, I know you were frightened last night," Willow said gently. "I'm sorry that happened. I'm also sorry you overheard about Rick Fenrow's prison break. But you need to understand how much we love you. We aren't going to take any chances with you and Brittany, believe me."

"Do you think he's following us?"

"It doesn't seem possible he could know where we're going, but we've got Larry with us, just in case. He's keeping watch on us."

"You're scared of Rick Fenrow, too, aren't you?" Lucy asked.

Instead of denying it, Willow drew Lucy close and hugged her.

"Okay, ladies," Larry Bager said, his voice gruff. "There'll be time for heart-to-hearts later. Our flight's already boarding. Better pick up the pace."

Willow never answered Lucy's question, which meant the answer was yes. Why didn't grown-ups ever admit to kids when they were afraid?

Lucy thought she knew why. Mama used to say, "Why should I try to explain something to you when you can't possibly understand it, anyway? It's grown-up stuff, and you're a kid. If you try to be a grown-up before you're ready, you'll get stupid and mess everything up. So let me be the grown-up for a while longer, okay?"

Mama was really scared the morning before she died. When grown-ups got scared, it meant there was something to be afraid of.

Ray deliberately placed himself behind Ginger as they waited to board, and he noted how hard she was trying to ignore him. He smiled to himself every time he caught her watching him from the periphery of her vision.

Last year at this time, had they been in this same situation, Ginger would have already known how he had enjoyed his trip so far, what he intended to accomplish for the remainder of the trip, and what she could do to help facilitate his time in Hawaii.

She would also have gathered the same information about every other person traveling with her. Ordinarily. Even taking into account her awkwardness with him, she seemed distracted.

He turned to look at her, and their gazes met briefly. To his surprise, for a moment, she didn't look away. A ridge of worry formed between her brows.

"Ginger?" he asked softly. "Is something wrong?

Something besides just—" he held his palm up and waved it between the two of them "—just this."

She blinked, her golden-brown eyes clouding, then she glanced at the children who stood beside her and turned away.

Dark-haired, dark-eyed Lucy continued to study him as they boarded, as if he were an interesting mathematical equation on a school chalkboard.

When they reached their seats, Ray sat behind Ginger. He smiled and winked at Lucy, and she looked away.

Once again, Lucy had the window seat, and she seemed pleased with this. She had remained near an adult at all times, while watching her little sister with all the dedication of a prison guard. Ginger wasn't the only one who seemed distracted by something, though from the little Ray knew of Lucy, he wasn't sure if this was characteristic of her or not.

Ray glanced at Graham and Willow, sitting across the aisle from Ginger and the two little girls. Steve and Helen Courtney sat across the aisle from Ray, with Larry Bager and Preston Black in front of Graham and Willow. Someone had made a concerted effort to keep the family together. To Ray's surprise, no one joined him. He had three seats to himself.

A flight attendant handed Lucy and Brittany blankets and pillows. Lucy wrapped herself from head to foot with the blanket, and pushed a pillow beneath her, craning to see out the window as they took off.

Before they had reached cruising altitude, Ray saw Brittany lie across Ginger's lap, and Ginger's head lolled sideways. He wanted to nudge her and remind her of the crick she would have in her neck if she stayed that way for long.

He remembered flying with her to Belarus a couple of times, usually overnight flights. He could never understand the logic of traveling at night. It wasn't as if most people were going to sleep—at least, he never did. Ginger was one of the few people who seemed able to sleep anywhere, anytime. He never could.

Ginger always awakened with a stiff neck. On their second flight to Belarus, he'd given her a pillow to support her neck. She'd taken it with her on every trip after that. But she hadn't brought it with her this time.

He glanced toward Lucy, and saw her watching him through the crack between her seat and Ginger's. He grinned and winked at her, and she retreated back into her cocoon, hiding from the world. But why?

He unbuckled his seat belt and leaned over the seat in front of him, pressed the release and gently pushed Ginger's seat back the two inches the airlines allotted for stretching out. Not generous, but better than nothing.

At the movement, Brittany snuggled closer to Ginger's shoulder. Ginger's lips parted slightly.

Ray couldn't help watching her, moved by the vulnerability that sleep always brought. How he wished—

Her eyes opened. For a quick moment, her gaze remained tender, holding his, warming with the start of a smile.

Then those same eyes chilled, memory obviously returning. The moment ended, and Ray felt a sharp prick of sorrow.

"I didn't want you to get a crick in your neck," he explained, suddenly awkward.

She nodded, resettling. "Thank you." Her tone didn't invite further conversation.

He returned to his seat, once again saddened by the loss of their former closeness. He rebuked himself for this inability to let the past go, but logic wasn't a part of this relationship. Had it ever been?

Lucy's head popped over the top of her seat, and she stared at him, her gaze solemn.

"My name's Ray," he whispered.

She nodded, grimacing, as if to say, *Of course I knew that. Do you think I'm deaf?*

"I believe this must be your first flight," he said.

She didn't say anything, but her eyes widened.

"Do you like it so far?" he asked.

She hesitated, then whispered, "Why do you want to know?"

Her question surprised him. Not something he'd have expected an eight-year-old to ask. Then he remembered about her mother. Lucy was behaving like a child whose mother had left her and her sister at home alone at night, careful to avoid talking to strangers, in case someone asked her about her home life.

"I remember my first flight." Ray continued to whisper. "My uncle took me up when I was ten years old. He had his own airplane, and he knew I was afraid of heights, so he talked me through takeoff. I loved it immediately. He flew me over the whole town of Branson, where I grew up."

Lucy blinked at him. "Why are you telling *me* about it?"

Again, her response startled him. "So you won't be so afraid."

The blanket she'd worn over her head slid to her shoulders. "I'm not afraid of flying."

He leaned a little closer. "I can tell you're afraid of *something,* though."

She pulled the blanket back over her head.

"I saw how frightened you were back at the airport," Ray said a moment later. "You haven't relaxed since I first saw you in Springfield. Are you afraid to fly over the ocean?"

Lucy shook her head.

"I saw how tightly you held Brittany's hand as we boarded the plane."

"Jet. It's a jet."

"Oh, excuse me. You're right, of course."

"I know why you're trying to be nice to me," she said.

He raised his eyebrows.

"You're talking to me because you like Aunt Ginger, and you want her to like you."

Ray laughed, hoping his laughter didn't offend Lucy.

She smiled, as if pleased that she'd caused this kind of reaction.

"Something funny?" came Ginger's sleep-riddled voice.

"Sorry," he whispered.

Lucy intrigued Ray. She reminded him of one of the kids at the children's home he helped support in Columbia—the child with the abusive father. Ray knew Lucy had endured some hardships in her short childhood, as had Brittany.

More reason to do everything in his power to see to it that this experience was a good one for her.

Lucy wasn't the only one who appeared unable to relax. Graham, Willow, Ginger, Preston, and this unexpected wild card in the mix, Larry Bager, all seemed hyperwatchful of the children, and of the crowds around them at the airport.

Ray studied the reflection of Lucy's face as she gazed out the window. What was she thinking right now? Was she simply looking at the clouds, enjoying her first chance to observe them from above instead of below?

Or was something darker weighing on her mind?

"Lucy?" he said softly, unwilling to leave well enough alone.

A moment later, her head appeared over the top of the seat. She looked wary of him still. "How do you know our names? You said Brittany's name, too, when you talked to me awhile ago."

"Graham is one of my best friends, and he talks about you girls all the time."

"He does?"

"He sure does. He's very much looking forward to the adoption."

Her eyes filled with sudden, surprised interest, and he could tell she was trying not to smile. "If Graham is one of your best friends, then why doesn't Aunt Ginger like you, too?"

"Oh, well, that's another story entirely."

She tilted her head to one side and waited, as if ready to hear the story.

"I've got a lot of extra room back here," he said. "It's

going to be a long flight. Want to spread out a little? I'll let you have my window seat. That way Ginger and Brittany will have more room to relax and—"

"And you'll have time to charm her before we reach Hawaii," Ginger said from the seat beside Lucy.

Ray laughed again, though he could see he wouldn't have Lucy's company beside him on this flight.

SEVEN

Ginger braced herself against the compelling appeal of Ray's hearty belly laugh, which characterized him more than any other single trait. He had an innate ability to see humor in some of the darkest situations, and that very asset had served him well over the years—had served everyone under his direction.

She unbuckled her seat belt and eased Brittany's head from her lap. With a reassuring pat on Lucy's hand, she slid to the aisle, allowing Brittany to stretch across both seats.

Ray stopped laughing when she plopped into the aisle seat beside him.

How could she have forgotten how much space this man took up? And that with barely an ounce of fat on him. Okay, maybe a few ounces. A man in a sedentary job didn't make it to forty-nine years old without acquiring a little added padding.

"We need to get a few things straight, Ray Clyde." Ginger kept her voice low, aware that Ray wasn't the only one whose attention had suddenly focused on her.

She could see Willow and Graham watching her from across the aisle.

She shot Graham a mind-your-own-business look, and he averted his gaze. Willow did not. Instead, she raised an eyebrow as if to warn Ginger to be good.

"What is it we need to get straight?" Ray asked.

She turned to find herself gazing up into eyes of the softest, darkest blue. How could someone with such a gentle gaze be able to make such cruel decisions?

"These two little girls are precious to me," she said quietly. "As they are to Graham and Willow. They've been through a lot of pain in their lives."

"I understand that. Graham told me."

"No, I'm not sure you *do* understand. They don't need to be used as pawns so you can try to make amends with me."

There was a slight hesitation, then, "You know better." His voice chided, but remained gentle, maybe a little sad.

In spite of herself—in spite of the truth that had lived with her since last March—she felt the sting of reprimand. She knew how much Ray loved kids. Helping children in need was his passion in life. As a pediatrician, he had access to all kinds of troubled children in Central Missouri, and while keeping up with a busy practice and overseeing GlobeMed, he also provided medical services free of charge for two orphanages in Central Missouri.

The knowledge that she wasn't earning any points with him—nor was she scoring points against him—didn't concern her. The only concern she had was that he not involve himself in Lucy's and Brittany's lives. They could easily attach themselves to him on this trip, then they'd be forced to endure yet another disappointment when it became obvious he wasn't going to be around any longer.

Yes, the girls could learn to live with another disappointment, but they'd had enough for a while.

It occurred to Ginger that she hadn't felt it necessary to warn Larry Bager not to form an attachment to the girls. Of course, Larry Bager didn't exactly strike her as a cuddly teddy bear of a man who would spend every waking moment with Lucy and Brittany unless he had to...unless he was paid to do it.

Not that she felt Ray was a cuddly teddy bear of a man, either, but...

"Let's try to be honest with one another for a moment," Ray said. "You feel you need to place some distance between the two of us on this trip, and so you must make sure I don't bond with Lucy or Brittany."

She leveled a look at him. He had that unnerving ability to read situations with quick conciseness. It wouldn't help to dissemble. She'd noticed he was no longer laughing.

"You have a problem with that?" she asked.

"I do. A considerable amount, as a matter of fact."

"Sorry you feel that way, but since I'm their caretaker on this trip, and I'm to be their Aunt Ginger, then I say what goes." What she wanted to say was for him to go home as soon as the wedding was over and leave all of them in peace.

But she knew that having another physically dominant male around to help watch out for the kids was probably a good idea, as much as she hated to admit it.

"I know you have a mind of your own," she said. "And I have no right to tell you what you can and cannot do with your time after tomorrow."

She really didn't want it involving her and the girls.

He watched her in silence, studying her expression, looking into her eyes, waiting.

She shifted in her seat. No one else had quite the same knack of rendering her speechless and making her feel like a total incompetent. But of course, that was his specialty, wasn't it? Making someone feel incompetent by removing that person from a loved post…

Stop it, Ginger. You're behaving poorly.

But hadn't Ray already drawn the battle line many months ago? And hadn't he crossed it first by coming on this trip?

How could Graham place her in this kind of situation?

"Ginger," Ray said, "we need to talk."

"That's what we're doing. Were you in on the double cross with Graham and Willow?"

"What are you calling a double cross?" His voice was a little too loud, and she saw Willow glance her way.

Ignoring the narrowed eyes of her friend, Ginger returned her attention to Ray. "Do you mind not dragging the whole cabin of passengers into this mess?"

"I'm not the one who—"

"Graham knows how the loss of my post in Minsk affected me. He brought you along, anyway."

"Maybe he thinks you overreacted last year and is trying to help you see that."

Ginger bit her tongue for a moment. Lucy would be listening carefully.

"Look, I realize this trip isn't about me," she said. "It must seem as if I'm behaving selfishly."

"I know you better than that," he said. "Under normal circumstances, you wouldn't behave this way."

She paused, trying to detect even a hint of sarcasm in his voice. "And besides," she said, "Graham and Willow have a right to anyone they want at their wedding."

"Exactly."

She bristled. He didn't have to be so smug about it. "But perhaps both my brother and my *former* mission director fail to see what your actions did to my life."

Ray blinked then, and she thought she detected a brief flicker of pain. Must be imagining things.

"I had children at that clinic whom I'd promised I'd return to," she said. "How must they feel about Christian Americans who aren't true to their word?"

"I explained your situation when I flew there," Ray said.

She remembered the edge of desperate appeal with which she had fought for a chance to return after her medical leave last year. She must have seemed to him to have an unhealthy attachment to her post. Was that the real reason he'd pulled her? Had he imagined some form of emotional instability?

"I have no doubt that it hurt you, Ginger," he said, "but that wasn't my intent."

"You don't have any idea what it did to me, and it's become obvious to me that neither does Graham, or he wouldn't have placed us both in this situation," she said, gesturing around them. Of all things, not only to place them together for the first time since their sharp disagreement last year, but to do so in such a public place?

"I think he knew what he was doing," Ray said.

She crossed her arms, feeling a wave of discomfort tingle her skin. "All right, then. He's a big boy, and this isn't his first marriage, or Willow's, so there's no need for a crowd of well-wishers. He could have had this wedding without his big sister holding his hand. After all, neither set of parents is coming with us."

"Maybe that's why it was so important for us to be here."

"If it had been so important to have you be his best man, I didn't need to be a part of it."

She knew she sounded childish, but right now the flow of words was covering up another, more immediate concern as another uncomfortable wave of heat rushed over her skin. Soon her face would flush bright red, and she would perspire.

Oh, Lord, please. Not now. How humiliating.

"That isn't fair." Ray's voice was a little harder this time. "Graham knows more than you do about the situation."

She blinked, surprised. "Why is that?"

He looked away. "He was aware of your health problems."

"So? I'm a physician's assistant, Ray. I understood your concerns. What more could he have known that I didn't? And why on earth wouldn't you tell me everything you told him? The condition was benign."

Ray gave a long, low sigh. "Let's just say Graham understood my concerns better than you did because he was also concerned. You have a tendency to think you're invincible. Those who know you and love you aren't always quite so cavalier about your safety."

"Meaning what?" she asked. "That I can't be trusted to take care of myself? That's silly. Besides, Graham wasn't the one being tricked to come back to the States. In fact, he helped you to coerce me back here."

"And yet you forgave him," Ray said softly.

More heat across her skin, more perspiration prickling her neck and chest. She resisted the urge to grab a magazine from the seat back in front of her and fan herself. "I know my brother. He was simply concerned for my welfare."

"And you couldn't accept the possibility that it was my concern, as well?" Ray asked.

"It seems to me your biggest concern was getting me out of Belarus and off GlobeMed's payroll so someone younger, with more training, could take my place. Yet you didn't have the guts to tell me the truth."

"You don't know what your future would have been if you'd stayed in Belarus," Ray said sharply. "A health problem that is benign here in America may not be so benign in a country that doesn't have the degree of health care that we have here in the States."

"We had everything we needed right in that clinic."

"Oh, sure, all the old equipment handed over by hospitals that were upgrading here in America. Half that equipment is useless, and there's no one in all of Belarus who knows how to repair those machines when they break down."

She frowned at him. There was something else going

on here that she wasn't quite grasping, and right now her discomfort was to the point that she didn't feel she could pursue it. *Get out now, Ginger, while you have some self-respect left.*

She waited for the flight attendants to pass with the refreshment cart, irritated that Ray was right. For the moment, she deemed it wise to discontinue the conversation. But when would she ever be able to discuss it without getting upset? One more thing she needed to say to him…

She leaned closer. "I doubt even Graham knows everything, Ray," she said, her voice lowered even further. "Such as the fact that you blocked me from returning to Belarus for even a two-year assignment with another mission board."

He looked disconcerted, and she felt a pang of sorrow. So it *had* been him. "You refused to give them a recommendation. Don't try to tell me this isn't personal."

Dripping with perspiration, and sure that Ray probably thought the perspiration and flushing came from anger, she returned to her seat.

As she shifted Brittany's sleeping form to once again rest on her lap, Ginger took a few deep, cleansing breaths and tried to think of icy mountain streams. The image would help her cool down not only her body, but also her thoughts.

The whole atmosphere of the wedding could be one of ugliness and petty fighting if she didn't do something to clamp down on this present, nasty mood.

She could control this.

* * *

Ray watched the back of Ginger's seat in frustration and deep disappointment. How could she have known him all these years and believe he would make such a decision about her life with cold, heartless calculation? When had she suddenly stopped trusting him?

He glanced across the aisle at Graham, who shrugged and shook his head, then mouthed the words, "Give it time."

But how much time would Ginger need? In three months it would be a year since she'd been forced home.

Was he being a coward for not coming clean with her about the real reason for bringing her back? She would never understand that the qualities about her that made him admire her were the same qualities that made her unfit for that particular post, in that particular country. She was right, even Graham didn't know everything, but it wouldn't have mattered. Graham trusted him. Ginger obviously didn't.

"Aunt Ginger?" Lucy whispered from in front of him.

"Yes?" Still a trace of anger there. And fatigue. Funny, he hadn't picked up on that sooner.

"Are you mad at me?"

"Of course not, sweetheart. Why would I be mad at you?"

Ashamed of himself, yet unable to resist, Ray strained to hear more.

"Your face is all red, like Mama's used to get when she was mad."

"Well, I'm not mad at you, so you can relax."

There was a moment of silence, then, "It's okay. You don't smack my face when you're mad."

"Now, why would I do that?"

No answer.

A moment later, Lucy spoke again, this time so softly Ray almost couldn't hear. "Aunt Ginger, why are you sweating? Your shirt's wet."

No answer. Only a tired sigh.

"Is Ray your boyfriend?"

There was a gasp of surprise. "What on earth would make you say something like that?"

"Because you were fighting. Mama always fought with her boyfriends. She used to say that they weren't worth loving if they weren't worth fighting with."

If Ray were to judge by the ensuing silence, he would conclude that Ginger was having as much trouble as he was deciphering that piece of twisted logic.

"I'm sorry, Lucy. I'm not behaving the way a grown-up should behave. You shouldn't think badly of Ray just because he and I don't see eye to eye about some things."

"I won't."

"Not even some important things."

"Okay."

"People can disagree."

"So you don't love him?"

"What?"

"Mama used to say she fought most with the boy-friends she loved the most. I guess some of them really loved her, because I think they hit her."

"Well, honey, that isn't the case today. Trust me."

"Mama says the making up is fun, though."

Ginger didn't remark on that.

"Do you think the making up will be fun?" Lucy asked in what she probably believed to be her most grown-up voice.

Ray couldn't help himself. He laughed again—out loud—and immediately realized he'd just given Ginger Carpenter another good reason to be angry with him.

EIGHT

Ginger changed the time on her watch, then peered over Lucy's head at the island as it came into view. Kauai. The Garden Isle. Nothing but green everywhere she looked. Beautiful beaches, flowers, rich, lush forests. Though the smallest of the four major islands, Kauai truly earned its name as the Garden Isle.

Ginger wanted to immerse herself in that garden and escape everything else. Unfortunately, that was not to be for a while.

Lucy stirred beside her, yawning.

"Have a look, my dear," Ginger said softly, cupping the child's chin and lifting it to encourage her to peer outside.

Lucy gasped aloud.

"Isn't it beautiful?" Ginger asked.

"Oh," Lucy whispered. "It's green everywhere! And it's so big. I thought islands were little."

"Compared to Missouri, this island is tiny. You know how far it is to drive from Hideaway to Springfield? This island isn't as long as that. And it's even narrower than that. About the distance from Branson to Ozark."

"Sounds big to me," Lucy said.

"It sure doesn't look like Missouri looks right now, does it?"

"It doesn't look like winter."

"It is. It just isn't like our winters in Missouri."

"Will it be cold, then?" Lucy asked.

"It may seem cold to the people who live here, but to us it'll be like springtime. They aren't used to really cold winters."

Ginger had been to most states in the U.S. She'd traveled halfway across the world several times to Belarus, with stopovers in England and Austria, and she'd taken road trips through Germany, Italy and Switzerland. She'd toured the Armory on Red Square in Moscow, and had been to the war memorial in Brest, Belarus—an awesome experience. She'd learned to love the Russian and Belarusian music, richly evocative of the passion of the people she'd also come to love.

In spite of her journeys, though, she'd never considered herself a world traveler. She'd never been west of California until now.

For weeks, as this trip was being planned, she'd immersed herself in Hawaiian music and history. She had studied the brochures Graham collected from the Courtneys. Ginger wanted to do it all.

What she would be doing, however, was watching the children. No downhill bike rides from Waimea Canyon for her. She would never dream of risking the girls' lives on a busy highway like that. No surfing, either.

Well, okay. Maybe if she could get Preston and Larry Bager to watch the girls, she would rent a surfboard and try her hand—or rather, her derriere—at the sport. Especially now that she'd lost twenty-five pounds on her heart-healthy diet. And she'd like to go snorkeling, if the water was warm enough. The girls would love that. She would surely be able to take them hiking.

Of course, Preston' and Larry both had already expressed their reluctance to take a hike in Koke'e State Park, so she was on her own there. She wasn't concerned about taking the girls out into the wilderness, however. As long as she made sure no one followed her there, she wouldn't have to worry about Rick Fenrow. It was the more public places where there was a greater need to keep watch, because Rick could blend in with the crowds.

As the jet moved into position for landing, Lucy's expression grew pensive once again.

"Don't worry so much," Ginger said. "We're not going to let anything happen to you."

Lucy looked up at her with eyes a little puffy from sleep. "Mama said she wasn't going to let anything happen to us last year, but then something happened to *her.*"

Ginger winced. She knew better than to make promises she didn't know she could keep. She'd learned that the hard way last year. But what could happen on an island in paradise?

Lucy held tightly to Brittany's hand as they left the jet and walked into the airport. The first thing she noticed was flowers. Everyone wore brightly colored clothes with flowers. There were flower necklaces around their necks, and people wore shorts.

Shorts in January. Didn't their mothers teach them how to dress?

A woman in a flower-print dress and long, black hair greeted them and gave them all flower necklaces.

Lucy couldn't help it, she held her breath when the woman wrapped the leis—that's what she called them—around Lucy's and Brittany's necks. Strangers scared her, even here, so far away from Missouri.

Helen and Steve led the group toward the baggage claim area, and Helen took Brittany's other hand.

Lucy watched the woman. On the jet, she'd kept trying to talk to Brittany across the aisle, asking her questions about school and her plans for their time in Hawaii, and taking pictures of her.

A few times, Lucy would look over to find Helen or Steve watching her and Brittany. As if they'd never seen kids before. Why were they acting that way?

Brittany pulled away from Lucy to go find the ladies' room. Lucy tried to call her back, but Helen said she'd take care of her, and followed her away.

When Lucy tried to go after her, Willow took her hand. "I need you to help us with suitcases, okay?"

"But I've got to go with them. I can't—"

"Shh-shh." Willow leaned over and brushed Lucy's hair back from her face with a gentle touch—a touch Lucy loved. "Listen to me, sweetheart. I know you've always taken responsibility for your sister, but on this trip you're here to enjoy yourself. Do you understand?"

Lucy didn't. Not exactly. But she nodded anyway, because she knew that was what Willow wanted.

"We have enough adults here to care for and keep watch over you and Brittany. You need to try to be a kid for once. Got that?"

Lucy hesitated, looking toward the bathroom door. "Do you know Helen?"

"She's a professional photographer who has planned a lot of exotic wedding trips like this one. She and Steve know a little about our circumstances, so they know to be on the lookout for anyone who behaves the least bit strangely."

"Okay."

Willow hesitated, and those lines formed above her eyebrows that Lucy only saw when Willow was trying to think about the best way to say something Lucy didn't want to hear. "Honey, you need to trust Graham and me, okay? I know that's a hard thing for you to do, but someday you're going to see that we know how to be parents. Please trust us a little bit more when it comes to Brittany, too. We aren't going to let anything happen to either of you, and we don't need our authority undermined."

"But I'm not trying to do that." She paused. "What does undermined mean?"

Willow grinned and hugged Lucy. "It means not letting the boss be the boss. The only person you have any reason to fear hasn't shown up. Steve and Helen are simply here to make our trip and the wedding all flow smoothly. Okay?"

"Okay. But can I go to the bathroom, too? I didn't like the one on the jet."

Willow smiled and kissed her. "That's fine, honey. You go on. But remember, you're safe here."

Lucy wasn't sure she agreed. Mama had constantly told them stories about things she'd seen bad people do.

Mama was obviously right, too. There were a lot of bad people in the world. Maybe even in Hawaii.

As soon as Ginger stepped outside and breathed her first whiff of warm Hawaiian air, she was hooked. The airport, like the majority of the island's towns, was on the ocean, and she caught the scent of it, mingled with the fragrance of her lei and a faint whiff of something being grilled, perhaps barbecued.

Vivid green plant life of every variety greeted her gaze. The evening sky was a brilliant pink, peach and indigo, with silver clouds that surrounded the setting sun, outlining it in elaborate beauty. Flowers of every color and shape overwhelmed her senses, and it seemed as if Kauai must be a haven for birds. Some she recognized. Some she certainly did not.

However, it was the wandering, pecking bantam chickens beneath the shrubbery that arrested her attention. Banties? Colorful farm poultry—so abundant in the Missouri Ozarks—running wild on a tropical island? What was that about?

Ginger glanced over her shoulder to see Lucy and Brittany safely under the care of Graham, Willow and Larry, awaiting the arrival of their guides with the rental vehicles. She couldn't resist a quick stroll along the sidewalk.

A rooster crowed barely a few feet from her, and she started, surprised to find that, even surrounded by all this overwhelming beauty, Lucy's hyperwatchfulness was affecting her.

Definitely time to relax a little. She was far removed

from all that had taken place in Missouri, and Larry was on the job.

She stepped from beneath the canopy that stretched between the airport and the car rental kiosk, and raised her face to the mellow golden glow of the setting sun. The island breeze played with strands of her hair, and she longed to sink her toes into the sandy beach.

"It wouldn't take much to convince me to live here." The deep voice behind her gave her a start.

She nearly stumbled from the edge of the sidewalk.

"Careful." Strong hands caught her and steadied her.

She grimaced and looked up into Preston Black's blue-gray eyes, so much like his sister's. "You don't have to sneak up on me like that."

"I wasn't sneaking." He released her and fell into step beside her. "Freaked about the prison break, aren't you?"

"I'm trying hard not to be."

"It's all anyone can think about." He shoved his hands into the pockets of his jeans. "That and your feud with Ray."

He wore an orchid lei over a pastel blue sweater that had been practical in Missouri, but definitely didn't seem appropriate now. He'd pushed the sleeves up to his elbows, revealing well-developed forearms that matched the rest of his buff physique.

Besides the blue-gray eyes, Preston had other features like his sister's—dark hair and dark, well-defined brows that made him look as though he was always brooding. He had a long face, firm chin, and a quiet watchfulness— even a thoughtfulness—that belied his macho image.

"I don't want to think about it," Ginger said. "Not

here. Not now. This time is for Graham and Willow. We should be focused on the wedding tomorrow."

Preston gave her a side-glance. "That's what the wedding planners are *supposed* to be taking care of."

"It seems that's what they're doing."

He shrugged. "Not sure what a wedding planner's supposed to do. Guess I've got a suspicious nature, but they were the ones who approached Mrs. Engle about this trip in the first place."

"How do you know that?"

"Mrs. Engle told me last week."

"Why would she mention something like that out of the blue?" Ginger asked.

"I asked."

Ginger gave him a pointed look. "Have you been trying to do Larry's job?"

"Not necessarily, I just got curious."

"Sure you did."

"I know Mrs. Engle has more money than we ever realized," he said, "but she didn't get rich by throwing her money away. I couldn't understand why she would hire someone to fly here with us when we're all perfectly capable of taking care of arrangements ourselves."

"A wedding trip like this needs a little more direction. Not only do we need a wedding coordinator, but someone who knows how to make everything run smoothly. Remember, to quote Helen, 'We're making memories to last a lifetime.' "

"Yeah, sure, but for two people to fly here, drive us around, take pictures? There's only seven of us, and one was tacked on at the last minute," he said. "So I got curious, did some checking. Do you realize this package trip is costing Mrs. Engle less than it would have if we'd made the arrangements ourselves?"

"That's why they call it a deal, Preston."

"Well, I didn't know what kind of deal it was, and I wanted to make sure we didn't get here and end up sleeping on the beach or something. Remember that plumber I started to hire last summer to update my rental? If I hadn't checked him out with the Better Business Bureau, I'd have been out a lot of money on that crook, and our pipes could've busted this winter."

Preston glanced over his shoulder toward Lucy and Brittany. Ginger followed his gaze, and she smiled. For once, even Lucy was distracted from her hyperalert state as she played with her lei.

"Think about it," Preston said softly. "Those little girls will be our nieces this time next week."

"It's an awesome thought," Ginger agreed.

He turned, strolled further. "My sister lost a baby three years ago because of Rick Fenrow, and I blame myself."

"That's silly. You didn't cause the miscarriage."

"I didn't believe her when she said she was being stalked. I thought the grief of losing her husband was affecting her mind, or that she was showing signs of our mother's schizophrenia. When it did happen—when Fenrow attacked her—I wasn't there for her. I'll never forget the feeling of loss and guilt when I discovered she'd lost the baby. If I'd been there…." He shook his head.

Ginger understood.

"When Willow moved in with me last year," he said, "I was determined nothing else would happen to her."

"You can't protect her from everything, Preston."

"Neither of us ever dreamed that man would burn my cabin and try to kill both of us."

"You can't predict evil," Ginger said.

"I plan to try. Nothing's going to happen to Lucy and Brittany if I can do anything to stop it."

"I know exactly how you feel," Ginger said. She resisted the urge to remind him that he was only human. She also resisted the urge to tell him to pray. Preston Black was going through an antireligious phase, which, according to Willow, had lasted most of his adult life.

"Do you have some reason to suspect that the girls could possibly be at risk from the wedding escorts, of all people?" Ginger asked.

"None. As they told Mrs. Engle, they've had several years' experience, and they've been to Hawaii often." He shrugged again. "They don't seem confident about this trip, and that makes me nervous. Helen's definitely a good photographer, but I saw her and Steve arguing in the airport in St. Louis."

Ginger smirked at him. "That's it? You suspect them because they argued?"

He gave her a dirty look. "Then both of them got on their cell phones and started making calls. They kept watching the rest of us, as if to make sure we couldn't overhear."

"Sounds like a glitch to me. Glitches can happen to the best of us, Preston, you know that."

He grimaced. "Don't I know it. Glitches like prison breaks."

She shook her head. "Don't even go there."

"Rick Fenrow is his father's son, after all. He's likely to have a whole file drawer filled with his father's old contacts."

"Where would that file drawer be?" she asked. "The FBI confiscated everything long ago, and his father is dead. Contacts go away. Quit being so suspicious, or Lucy will pick up on it, and you know she'll be impossible to reassure."

"People who moved on the wrong side of the law two years ago will still be there," Preston said. "They'll know how to get things done and successfully avoid the radar of the police."

Ginger closed her eyes briefly. "You had to remind me."

"Fenrow's the son of a dirty attorney. He grew up knowing the tricks of his father's trade. All he'd have to do would be to make one phone call."

"But he doesn't know where we are and what we're doing, does he?"

Preston shrugged. "We have no way of knowing how much information he might have."

"Okay, but don't you think he'd be more concerned with a few more important things?" Ginger asked. "Things like going underground to keep from being apprehended, and staying hidden?"

"That guy has lived with the need for revenge. I don't think prison would have changed him. If anything, it would have fueled the fire."

Ginger rolled her eyes at his dramatic tone. Preston tended to be pessimistic. But she couldn't figure out why he was so negative right now.

"Uh, Preston? Is something up with you?"

"What do you mean? We've got a killer on the loose. How much worse can it get?"

"Oh, I don't know, maybe some concern about a certain girlfriend named Sheila, left behind in Branson, who actually did have some experience working with Rick when he was disguised as a nice human being. Are you worried he might try to make some kind of contact with her?"

He walked a few seconds in silence. "She knows what he looks like, and she's aware of the prison break now."

"So you've been in contact with her?" Ginger hinted.

"I called her. We talked. She's not the least bit concerned about an escaped killer. She has other things on her mind."

Ginger turned to him. "Those other things couldn't possibly be romance with one of the most eligible men in Branson, could it?"

He smiled, but the smile was forced. "I said I'd been in contact with her, not that we'd set a wedding date. Would you back down a little?"

She studied his expression, comparing it with the goofy grin that had lit his face a few weeks ago whenever Sheila's name was mentioned. "Everything's okay, isn't it?"

He hesitated. "Let's say I'm pretty sure she likes me, beyond that is anyone's guess right now."

Ginger backed off. She knew Preston well enough to know something was bothering him, and that he wouldn't talk about it until he was in the mood. He didn't often get into the mood for those kinds of confidences.

Preston Black was what most women of Ginger's generation called a hunk. Or, at least, it was what Ginger called him. But she could get away with teasing him about his looks from time to time. At thirty-eight, he was sixteen years younger than she.

Of course, he was older than his sister, Willow, by two years, and he used that advantage to boss her around sometimes—or rather, he tried. Ginger hoped that wasn't the problem between him and Sheila.

His sister gave as well as she got, and often better. Willow never allowed anyone to push her around, as Ginger had discovered ten minutes after meeting her. Ginger had picked up quickly on Willow's independence, and had respected it, for the most part.

Preston, on the other hand, was his most aggressive when with his sister, and he never seemed to notice when his occasionally overbearing attitude chafed Willow. Perhaps Willow should give her big brother a talking-to, if he was trying the same tactics with Sheila.

Why were men so obtuse about some things?

From the comfortable age of fifty-three, Ginger could observe those male-female games with amusement and fond memories…at least, most of the memories were fond.

She shot a look over her shoulder toward Ray, who stood slightly apart from the rest of the happy family and Larry, their bodyguard. Ray Clyde had a few lessons to learn about women, as well.

"I hate to change the subject, Preston, but when did the switch take place for best man at the wedding?"

He chuckled, raising his hands. "Oh, no you don't. You're not dragging me into this battle."

"There's no battle."

"Could've fooled me, watching you with Ray on the flight today."

"This whole thing could have been handled so much better if I'd had some kind of warning. As it was, I didn't know Ray was coming until I saw him boarding the jet. Is there any wonder why I felt duped?"

"Well, you'd better stop blaming your poor brother," Preston said. "The whole thing was my idea."

Ginger gasped. "Young man, you're as devious and conniving as Graham!"

He chuckled, his deep laugh attracting the attention of a couple of women seated at a bench, who eyed him with interest.

It was characteristic of him that he didn't notice. He threw an arm over Ginger's shoulders. "I've never seen you in a situation you didn't know how to deal with. This should prove interesting, as long as you don't kill the best man before the wedding."

NINE

Ray couldn't prevent the jealousy that pierced him as he watched Ginger and Preston Black together, particularly when Preston put his arm around Ginger.

Yes, the man was probably quite a few years younger than Ginger, but she was a young fifty-three. Ray, himself, was forty-nine. He had discovered years ago that an age difference no longer served as a deterrent to an otherwise promising relationship.

Ray had only met Preston a few weeks ago, and had immediately liked him. Preston was like his sister— honest, serious, earnest—exactly the kind of person Ginger would adore.

Of course, it felt to Ray as if Ginger would be likely to adore anyone but him right now.

Willow stepped to Ray's side and touched his arm. "Didn't you and Ginger manage to talk things out on the flight here?"

"She isn't open to anything I have to say right now."

"It's all right," Willow said softly, as if soothing an upset child. "I'm sure everything will be fine. Remember, she may threaten a lot of things, but she isn't dangerous in most situations."

"That's your opinion." He knew better. Ginger had the power to cause him a great deal of damage, just not in a way that would be visible to the naked eye.

"She's already caught up in the allure of the island," Willow said. "Give it time, Ray."

"I've done that."

"Let the peace and beauty of the island do their work on her."

"She's not likely to let her surroundings affect her memories to that extent," he said. "But I believe she'll be as polite as she can to keep from upsetting anyone else, particularly those two." He gestured to the children, who were busy comparing their leis and sniffing the flowers—for once, giggling like little girls.

"No. Of course, you're right." Willow placed a hand on Lucy's shoulder. "I don't know how Ginger will feel about it, but I really would appreciate your help with these two while we're here."

"I'd love nothing better, but I have to admit, I'm curious. Why the armada of adults to keep watch on two sweet little girls? Is there something about them I don't know? Such as, they turn into goblins after sunset, or something as hideous and scary?" How much effort could it take to keep an eye on Lucy and Brittany?

Graham joined the two of them, and Ray noted, as he had a couple of times on their flight, that his friend's typically serene expression was tight with a tension he seldom exhibited.

"Something else is up," Ray said, studying them both

more closely. It was the reason for Lucy's watchfulness, and possibly even the reason for some of Ginger's surliness, though he couldn't place much of the blame there.

"We received word late last night that Sandi Jameson's killer has escaped prison," Graham said.

Ray closed his eyes for a second, feeling the shock of the news like a blast of winter sleet. When he opened his eyes again, his gaze fell on the orphans whose mother had been killed by a deranged monster. "The police called to warn you?"

"No, actually," Willow said. "Larry Bager is a private investigator who used to work on the police force. He's the one who told Graham about it last night."

"Where was the prison?"

"Kansas."

Ray nodded. "I'm no expert, but I would consider it protocol for the prison to call those who might be affected by the prison break."

"They actually did call this morning before we left for the airport," Graham said. "I think the fact that Rick Fenrow was in a different state has something to do with the slow response time."

"So they haven't found him, yet." Ray shook his head.

"I'm glad Larry came with us," Graham said. "He was helpful last year."

"Didn't you say the killer went undercover to get to Willow?" Ray asked softly, making sure the girls were distracted.

"That he did," Graham said. "He put on a good disguise, working as an orderly at the hospital. Ironically, it was the hospital where Preston was taken for his injury in the fire, which Rick had set in the first place."

"Sounds like a great deal of hostility in that man," Ray said.

"That was directed toward me," Willow said, her voice quiet. Her blue-gray eyes darkened with the memory. "Others suffered for something I did."

"That's not true and you know it," Graham said, giving his fiancée a gentle nudge and a loving look. "You and others suffered because of an evil man."

"I've heard the general gist of that story, but never the whole thing." Ray risked another glance toward Ginger and Preston, saw them talking and smiling, with their heads together. He looked away.

"Several years ago Willow was working in ICU when Rick's father—an attorney for organized crime bosses—was brought into the hospital as an injured patient," Graham explained. "Under the influence of pain medication, Rick's father muttered information about a murder. Willow reported it to her husband, who was an undercover cop. The police force was put into motion because of Willow's information, and they found enough evidence on the attorney to put him in prison for quite some time."

"I think Rick might not have lost control so completely if his father hadn't developed Parkinson's disease while in prison," Willow said. "The progression of the man's condition was rapid."

"You're saying Rick blamed you for everything, Willow?" Ray asked.

"Isn't that typical of people who don't want to take responsibility for their own actions?" Willow asked.

"He abducted her," Graham said, keeping his voice soft so as not to alert the children to the seriousness of their conversation. "Before Willow could be rescued, Rick Fenrow shot her full of the same medication his father had been given in prison for his illness."

"Dopamine," Willow said. "An ironic and particularly frightening experience for me, because the drug can trigger psychotic responses in some people. Since I have a family history of schizophrenia, my reaction was horrible for one night, but it didn't last."

Graham placed a loving arm around Willow's shoulders and drew her close. "She hasn't had a recurrence," he said with emphasis, as if he felt she needed a reminder of that fact.

Ray watched the two of them together, and felt a pang of yearning. He couldn't be happier for his old friend, but the obvious love between Graham and Willow made Ray wish for that same sense of belonging—something he had once mistakenly thought he might share with one fascinating woman who had a lot of love to offer.

"You think this killer might have managed to follow you all here?" Ray asked.

"I don't want to dismiss any possibility at this time," Graham said. "In spite of the improbability of it, he's resourceful."

"Why don't I hang around after the wedding awhile?" Ray suggested.

Graham gave him a smile of obvious relief and placed a hand on his shoulder. "I hate to ask it of you, considering the behavior I've seen in my sister today. I apologize."

"No need for that."

"I'll have a talk with her," Graham said.

"Don't you dare," Ray said. "She's already angry with me. If you insinuate yourself between the two of us, she would be hurt, I think. Worse than she already is."

"But Ray—"

"Don't even start. I know I did what needed to be done, but your sister had to protest it. That's the way she's made."

"Guess I can't argue with that," Graham said.

Ray shook his head. "Wouldn't do any good. We'll see how it goes in the next couple of days."

Preston sighed when Steve and Helen reappeared driving two vehicles. "Well, at least we do have two cars, though I was hoping for more cars for this group."

Ginger grinned at his lame attempt to change the subject from the wedding and Ray. "We can get a rental in Poipu easily enough, I'm sure."

"But what do we know about Poipu? As I said, I don't feel our guides are totally clued in. What if we get to Poipu and there's no car rental? We could be sleeping in tents for all we know."

"I doubt the Hyatt Regency has its rooms in tents," Ginger said dryly, "even on a tropical island in the middle of the Pacific. I think our escorts are doing a great job. They got us here, didn't they?"

Preston pointed toward the dark red Nissan Xterra and a silver-blue minivan, then turned to join the others. "Give them time. We'll see."

She followed him, chuckling to herself. Preston

Black was one of those macho guys who was currently building a cabin in the Hideaway woods on his own—from blueprints to decking. His former cabin had been burned to the ground last year, compliments of Rick Fenrow. Now, he had chosen Hideaway as a place to put down new roots. Literally.

He was far enough along on his project that he had moved into the cabin this past week. He would place the finishing touches on it when he returned from this trip.

Preston was a hunter and angler who had little use for a suit and tie now that he no longer worked as an accountant-financial advisor.

Ginger glanced at Ray to find him watching her, brooding. She had seldom seen Ray brood. She held his gaze for an uncomfortable moment, feeling a twinge of remorse for the way she'd spoken to him on the flight.

Willow was right; no use dragging everyone else into this battle.

Ginger knew it was time to paste on a smile and try to retrieve some of the ground she'd lost with her little temper tantrum-hot flash episode earlier. She and Ray didn't need to resurrect another major conflict, not with everything else that was going on right now.

Still, Graham needed to understand that his cavalier treatment of her feelings was unacceptable. That, too, however, was something that needed to wait until a more appropriate time.

She hoped for the sake of Willow and Graham that tomorrow's wedding went well. Neither set of their parents had been able to make it. Ginger and Graham's dad was recovering from surgery. Ginger had been to see him last week for Christmas. Willow and Preston's mother was having another bad episode with her schizophrenia. The Christmas season seemed to be the worst time of the year for those who suffered from emotional difficulties.

Helen and Steve Courtney helped everyone load their luggage into the vehicles. After consulting a map and speaking at length with one of the airport attendants, the group was on its way.

Preston sat in the backseat of the minivan with Ginger and Lucy. "See what I mean?" he muttered softly enough so the driver couldn't hear him. "Clueless."

Ginger gave him a teasing smack on the arm. "You're such a ray of sunshine today, Preston Black. I can't wait to see you snorkeling. Or maybe you'll take the girls and me hiking. Did you pack your hiking boots?"

"Do sandals count?"

"Oh, please, at least tell me you brought some tennis shoes."

He nodded. "And a swimsuit. I'm ready for anything."

"I'm glad we came here instead of going to another island. Kauai is the smallest and least developed of the main islands. Oahu and Maui attract more visitors, I think."

"Less likely for someone to find us?" Preston murmured softly.

Ginger nodded. "We'll be fine. I'm sure we'll be in Poipu in thirty minutes or less, and in our rooms soon after."

Ginger, Willow and the girls were to share a suite tonight as they prepared for tomorrow's wedding, and for the luau tomorrow night. Ginger was looking forward to some girl time this evening.

Graham would never have spent this kind of money on himself, especially now, with nearly everything he owned invested into the free clinic. For Willow, however, he would do anything. That had not been necessary when Mrs. Engle revealed her intentions.

Willow had once shared a secret with Mrs. Engle: she had always dreamed of a wedding at the Fern Grotto, on Wailua River. She'd read about it as a teenager, and from then on had hoped to someday see it. When Willow and Graham announced their engagement, Mrs. Engle had immediately decided what her wedding gift would be, and Willow had not been able to talk her out of it.

As Ginger and Preston rode in silence, Ginger watched Preston. He was a hard man to read. Though he liked to think of himself as a simple man of the land, she knew he had a quick wit and was a deep thinker. He seemed to be concerned about something right now.

Though she knew him well, and often thought of him as a younger brother, she couldn't read his mind the way she often could Graham's.

Helen suddenly slammed on the brakes and groaned, then muttered to herself.

"What's wrong?" Ginger asked in alarm.

"It's okay, don't worry," Helen said, her voice sounding falsely bright. "Just missed a turn in the dark. I think. Not a lot of signs along this section of highway, are there? The lady at the car rental desk warned us that some of the signs had been blown away by a tropical storm some time ago, and they haven't all been replaced yet."

Graham gave a whistle of amazement from the front passenger seat. "That sounds like quite a storm. Didn't I hear someone at the airport mention there might be another one brewing in the next couple of days a little east of here?"

Helen gave him a brief glance. "We've been watching that one."

"And?" Graham prompted.

"Hawaii seldom gets hit by storms, so we weren't worried about it, especially since it wasn't supposed to come in this direction. We learned a few hours ago that it's turning. Steve and I made some calls. It doesn't seem to be much of a threat, even if it does come our way."

Ginger nudged Preston, and he winked at her. That must have been what the concerned looks and quick phone calls were about at the airport.

"Settle back and relax, folks," Helen said as she turned onto what Ginger hoped would be the correct road. "We'll be in Poipu in no time."

Lucy reached for Ginger's hand and held on tightly. Brittany woke up and started to whimper in the seat in front of them. Willow murmured words of soothing comfort.

Another wave of heat moved over Ginger's skin. She grabbed a brochure she'd picked up at the airport to fan herself. This promised to be a long week.

TEN

Almost as soon as Ray climbed into the SUV with Steve Courtney at the wheel, he realized the man did not know his way around the town of Lihue. After fifteen minutes, Ray realized that Steve most likely had never even been on Kauai before, and if he had, it had been daylight.

Not that Ray could have done much better, considering the paucity of road signs. And the few that were posted did not match the directions he'd overheard at the airport.

The caravan arrived at the Hyatt Regency in Poipu a full ninety minutes after leaving the airport. Ray was ready for bed.

Larry Bager cleared his throat from the backseat when Steve, going in the wrong direction, pulled into a one-way drive in the hotel complex. "Not from around here, are you?" the P.I. asked in a perfect impersonation of an Ozark backwoodsman.

Steve chuckled uneasily. "This isn't one of our regular tours."

"You don't say," Larry said drily. "You're sure our group has reservations at this hotel?"

"Of course I am." Steve found the bellman's stand and parked beside it. "There's only one Hyatt Regency in Poipu, and I have our confirmations in my briefcase."

"Didn't I hear someone say that the drive from the airport to Poipu took thirty minutes?" Larry asked.

"Obviously, that would be for someone familiar with the road system. Sorry about those little detours. They would have been much prettier during daylight, I'm sure."

"So, how many groups have you brought here in the past?" Larry asked.

"Actually, this is our first stay at the Hyatt-Regency," Steve said as he opened his door. "Helen and I typically take our Hawaii tours to Maui, Oahu and the Big Island. To be honest, we've never driven to Poipu in the dark, and in case you hadn't noticed, the signs aren't the best right now."

Helen met Steve as he stepped out. The woman had a youthful prettiness that belied her years—which Ray had heard was in the low sixties. Right now she looked drawn and pale.

"I received a call from Wedding Dreams on my cell. We can't get a boat into Fern Grotto tomorrow."

For several seconds, Steve was silent. Then he sighed heavily. "Why not? We booked it weeks ago."

"The company's worried about the storm," she said softly.

"We were told that wouldn't be a problem," Steve snapped.

Larry leaned over and looked out at Helen. "I heard that little tropical depression was going to miss Hawaii."

Helen shrugged. "It's changed course, apparently,

but from all accounts, even if it does reach us here, that shouldn't happen for about twenty-four hours."

"What about another company?" Steve asked. "Can that be so difficult? It's off season."

Helen shrugged. "I asked them if they couldn't find something for us with another outfit, but there's a convention in town. It seems the Fern Grotto is popular."

Steve sighed heavily. "This is just great."

"I'm sorry," Helen said, drawing him away from the SUV, lowering her voice. Ray could only hear snatches of what she said. "...don't know what else...whom to call on this island. Willow and Graham aren't too worried...do some shopping tomorrow...can't let yourself get worked up...heart isn't as strong..."

When Steve and Helen returned to help the bellman unload the vehicles, Larry drew Ray aside.

"I don't like this," he grumbled.

"I'm not crazy about it, either, but if Graham and Willow are okay waiting another day, it shouldn't make any difference to us."

"You heard what Steve said. A tropical storm brewing, and our guides aren't familiar with the island?" He shook his head. "I don't have a good feeling about it."

"What do you propose we do? It isn't as if there's a hurricane coming this way. We'll get a little rain for a day or two, stay inside and read or watch movies."

"I think I'll have a look at the weather channel once we get to our rooms."

"I don't know how Helen and Steve were able to get flights and room reservations for you at such short notice," Ray said.

"They didn't. I got my own."

"Maybe you should become a tour guide."

Larry grimaced at him. "Funny. I'm two doors down from you and Preston. Willow, Ginger and the girls have a suite between us, and Graham is across the hall from you. There are probably still some of the holiday tourists here, judging by the number of cars we saw coming in."

"Some of the rich university crowd enjoying a few more days of warmth," Ray suggested.

Even as he spoke, a raucous group of twentysomethings came up from the beach, most wearing shorts, but with jackets and sweaters in deference to the cooling evening air.

Larry studied each new face as the party entered the lushly appointed hotel.

Ray had no doubt that if Larry Bager, P.I., had anything to do with it, the prison escapee would come nowhere near this wedding party. Awkward as this situation was, Ray liked knowing that someone was totally dedicated to the safety of this group.

The ocean waves beckoned to Ginger through the screen door that led out to the lanai of the luxurious two-bedroom suite. A few moments ago, the girls had stopped running from room to room, exclaiming at each new discovery of scented soaps, lotions, flower arrangements and snacks and drinks in the refrigerator.

At last, Ginger gave in to the call of the waves—at least from a distance. Though she had no doubt Larry Bager would read her the riot act if she attempted to go walking on the beach alone—thanks to the threat of one wicked person—she slipped on a sweater over her jeans and T-shirt and left Willow reading a story to the girls.

From where she stood on the fourth floor lanai, Ginger could see what she presumed to be Shipwreck Beach, sea foam and waves gleaming in the moonlight. The heady smell of ocean surf combined with the perfume of blooming flowers and created an unforgettable scent of which she knew she would never tire.

Ginger had loved the ocean from the first time she and her family had vacationed at Big Sur in her early childhood. Ever since, she'd tried to make it a point to see the pounding surf at least once every couple of years. It didn't happen often enough for her. The only way she could get enough of the ocean was to live by it.

Now, she had to fight her frustration with the new restrictions that were keeping her from the sea. How she would love to go splash barefoot in the water without having to worry about some madman attacking her. And now it looked as if the weather was not going to cooperate with them on this trip.

But that was no way to look at things. God was always in control, both of the weather, and their protection. She'd learned that so many years ago. Why did it always seem so easy to lose the assurance of those lessons?

With a quiet sigh, she closed her eyes and leaned against the railing. Willow's deep, melodious voice rose and fell from the main room of their luxury suite, and mingled with the whisper of water on sand.

"I know exactly what you mean" came a deep voice from the darkness to her left. "It's breathtaking."

Her eyes flew open and she turned to see Ray Clyde in the shadows of the lanai next to hers.

Careful, Ginger. No smart retorts, the children might hear. She turned from the railing and reached for the sliding door.

"Please don't let me scare you away," Ray said. "That wasn't why I—"

"You're not." She slid the screen door open and reached for the glass one, then slid it shut, being quiet so as not to disturb the story in which the girls were so engrossed.

From the glow of indoor light, she caught sight of Ray's expression of concern, and couldn't repress a quick grin. He, no doubt, was bracing himself for yet another verbal attack from her.

She refrained.

"I didn't come out here to fight with you," he said.

"Good, because I'm not up to battle stance for the next week, especially not with everything else going on." She sank into the deck chair farthest from Ray. "It's late, and it's been a long day. I want to listen to the surf in peace for a few minutes before I turn in." She hoped he could tell by her tone and her words that she hadn't expected, nor did she want, company.

"My thoughts exactly," he said.

"Good."

"Fine."

She shot him a quick look, then tilted her chair away from him.

Unfortunately, now that the company was nearby, he was all she could think about—much the same as it had been on the flight. It frustrated and irritated her that, even at the mature age of fifty-three, she behaved like a young, impressionable woman when it came to certain men.

Okay, when it came to Ray.

Worse, it had become obvious to her over the course of this day, as she thought about it, that she would not have been so unforgiving of anyone else who had forced her to leave her mission post. In fact, she wanted to think she would have been understanding.

What had cut her more deeply than anything last year was the knowledge that Ray Clyde, of all people, had believed her to be unfit to continue. Ray Clyde, whom she had considered for so many years to be a close friend and confidant, whose opinion and approval she had valued above that of almost anyone else, had rejected her. Not only had he rejected her, but he wouldn't even give a recommendation to another missionary board.

How much more obvious could he have been? He didn't value her professionally or personally. It wasn't something she'd wanted to admit to herself today, and she especially hoped she wouldn't blurt it out, or show her vulnerability in any other way.

But how was she supposed to smile and behave as if nothing was wrong?

Ray felt himself engulfed in a wave of sadness so poignant it marred the beauty of the evening, the softness of the breeze, the sweet scent of gardenia and plumeria that powdered the air with their delicate perfume.

Silence had never felt so barbed with anger and unspoken pain. In spite of Ginger's assurance that she just wanted peace, he couldn't let this opportunity pass without some kind of attempt at reconciliation—perhaps to bring about that peace that seemed to be evading her.

"Something about this trip has generated a lot of memories for me," he said at last, then continued without waiting for Ginger to comment. "Graham's put on a few years and a few pounds, but he has that same quiet strength about him, that determination to make sure that everyone in his care is happy."

She didn't reply, but continued to stare into the darkness.

"Even if he realizes they may have to struggle a little to get to that place of happiness," Ray continued. "He's always been the type to do what he felt was best, in spite of opposition."

"You're right, he hasn't changed a bit, but you sure have." She glanced his way, then returned to her study of the surf.

"How have I changed?" Ray asked.

A quiet sigh. "Ten years ago, if I'd told you I wanted some peace, you'd have left me alone."

"Ten years ago maybe I didn't know you as well as—"

"Don't start that. Didn't you hear me tell you I wasn't up to a fight?"

He gritted his teeth. "I'm not trying to fight, I'm trying to make peace so we won't feel compelled to fight the whole week. As we stand right now, we're both on edge constantly."

"Maybe you and Graham should have thought about

that before you sprang this surprise on me," Ginger pointed out.

"I think if you were happier with the job you're doing now, you wouldn't be so—"

"Don't you dare start with me." Her voice seemed to echo over the roar of the waves. "You of all people should know better. I *had* a job I loved until—"

"You're treating patients, Ginger. You're helping people. That should be as satisfying in Branson or Hideaway as it is anywhere else."

"Then obviously you don't know anything about it. Ever considered turning over your directorship to someone who understands foreign missionaries better?"

He winced inwardly at the sting in her words. He truly didn't want to argue, especially not with Ginger. "I can't imagine having to give it up."

"That's what I had to do, though, Ray, so why don't you try to imagine it for once. How would you have felt?"

"Why don't you tell me what's so different between meeting patient needs overseas, and meeting them here in America."

"You mean besides the fact that we Americans are spoiled beyond belief?" she asked. "That we take top-notch health care for granted?" She stood up and took a few steps across the lanai toward him. "That we've decided we have a God-given right to perfect, uninterrupted health care by people who must answer to our attorneys for the slightest sign of a slip?"

He winced at the heat behind her words. "Yes, besides that."

"Well, I guess none," she said, then added softly, "I want to help those who truly need the help."

"Graham mentioned some of your concerns."

"Did he also mention that I've struggled this past year to lose weight in deference to his pleas, in spite of the fact that my irregular heartbeats were totally harmless to begin with? I'm not ready to be put out to pasture."

"Of course you aren't."

"In fact," she continued, "I'm barely getting started. I deserve another chance, Ray."

"No one has ever denied you opportunities to serve, but you have always been dead set on serving at one particular place."

She leaned over the railing as if she would come across and grab him by the collar to make him see her reasoning. "Of course I have, I formed a bond with those people, with the kids especially. Sergei, Colya, Nick, so many that I watched grow from children to young adults. You know how close I was to Sergei, especially after his father died. I knew their language— and I'm not talking about the Belarusian language, I'm talking about the language of their hearts."

He felt another quickening of empathy for her. So much pain. *Oh, Ginger, if you only knew how sorry I am about all this.* "What makes you think you couldn't learn the language of another group in the same way?"

"Because that kind of a bond isn't formed overnight. Ray, I don't have to be director. I don't have to control the clinic, I need to see those children again. I need to be there to—"

He heard the self-reproach in her voice as it broke off.

He could tell that she suddenly realized she was begging. Again.

"Ginger, I never wanted to cause you pain, and if the decision hadn't been absolutely necessary, I never would have made it. I don't know how to convince you of that, but it's true." He was more than sorry. It broke his heart. But he would rather have his own heart broken than to see Ginger devastated further.

She was silent for too long. He could almost sense a change in the way she watched him, and he realized his voice had given him away.

"What are you neglecting to tell me?"

He closed his eyes. *Don't ask, Ginger. Please don't ask.*

"It isn't about my health anymore, is it?"

He didn't reply.

"Was it ever about my health?"

"Yes, it was." He could say that truthfully. Maybe not in the way she meant, but…

"Ray—"

The door of the lanai slid open and Willow stepped out. "Guess what? Helen found another boat to take us to the Fern Grotto tomorrow. Looks like we'll have some time for shopping in the morning, then a wedding tomorrow afternoon!" She clapped her hands together, excited as a young girl. "Let's get some sleep, okay?"

Ray sagged with relief, blessing Willow for the interruption. This promised to be a long, difficult week as things stood right now. He didn't hang around to see if Ginger would press their argument further. He slipped inside and went to bed.

ELEVEN

A tune played in Ginger's head through the heavy darkness. It mingled in harmony with the song of the waves through the screen of her open window. It was a catchy tune, with a great rhythm, one that made a person feel like dancing.

Then she awakened and opened her eyes. The tune continued to drift through the darkness. The illuminated numbers on her bedside clock told her it was four in the morning. The tune came from her purse on the padded bench at the end of her bed.

Someone was calling her on her cell phone.

She sat up as the tune ended. Why hadn't she turned that stupid thing off last night? In fact, why hadn't she left it at home? Nobody ever called her on it except Graham.

But Graham wouldn't be calling her now. He was fast asleep in his own room. Must be someone from back home, perhaps a wrong number.

Before she could drift back to sleep, she heard another sound come through the screened window. She knew it well. It was a rooster crowing.

"I don't believe this," she muttered, turning over in

bed and pulling the pillow around her ears. Roosters didn't crow at 4:00 a.m. in Hideaway.

Or maybe they did, and because she and Graham kept the windows closed at night, she'd never heard them before. Roosters crowed at lights. Not only the sunlight, but sometimes bright moonlight, or an electric light left on overnight. They must crow here on the shoreline a lot, with all the lights Ginger could see from her window.

The phone beeped to tell her that someone had left her a message. Then, before she could decide what to do, the music started again. The crowing grew louder. Obviously the crazy bird had strutted nearer to the window, hoping to compete with the sound of the cell phone.

With a sigh, Ginger got out of bed, longing for the earplugs she'd left at home.

Ray couldn't believe his ears, and when he looked at the clock, he couldn't believe his eyes. Four o'clock? What crazy rooster would crow at four in the morning?

Not that he was a country boy anymore. He hadn't lived on a farm since he'd graduated high school, but he knew roosters in Missouri at least had the decency to wait until the sun lightened the sky before they had the audacity to awaken people.

Another rooster joined the first, loud and close. Though Ray's room was on the fourth floor, the sound carried well. He imagined the rest of the wedding party might also have left their windows open. If they had, there would be some groggy people in the morning.

He slipped from bed and pulled on the clothes he'd

removed a few hours ago. Ginger was irritated enough with his presence on this trip. He hated to think what her attitude would be if she lost another night of sleep.

Graham and Willow deserved better for their wedding day.

Sliding his key card into the back pocket of his slacks, Ray stepped from the room and closed the door quietly behind him.

He was thinking about fried chicken for breakfast in a few more hours. The thought staved off some irritation.

Ginger frowned at the number and name on the lighted screen of her cell phone. She unfolded the silly thing and answered. "Taylor Jackson? Is that you? Why are you calling at this hour?"

"Sorry, Ginger, I didn't even think about the time difference, but this is kind of important." The deep voice carried across the miles with comfortable familiarity. "I tried to call Graham, but his cell phone is apparently turned off. I would have tried to find the number for the hotel next, but since I've got you, I'll talk to you."

"Please tell me this is just a friendly call to wish the bride and groom a happy wedding today."

"Uh, sorry. I mean, I do wish them a happy wedding, but this is official business."

"What's wrong?"

"Well, I hate to tell you this, but Blaze Farmer was doing chores over at your place earlier this morning, and he noticed something strange."

She stiffened. "Something like what?"

"Like we had about an inch of snow here late yesterday morning after you left, and he saw footprints around the side of the house, leading to the front door. So he used his key to go inside, especially after the excitement we had there the other night."

Oh. No. "What did he find?" she asked, afraid of what he would tell her.

"Sorry to say this, but it sure did look like somebody searched the house. Didn't you have a calendar on the kitchen wall beside the sink?"

"Yes. That's where I keep my monthly schedule."

"That's what Blaze said. Did you take it with you to Hawaii?"

"No, I brought a copy."

"It isn't there now. Did you have anything on it about your trip?"

"Sure I did. I marked off every day for a month, preparing for this trip. We had notes all over the house reminding us about what to pack. As it was, I forgot to pack Brittany's bear. Did you see any signs of forced entry?"

"None, but anyone with a few simple mechanical skills could pick the locks easily enough. It isn't as if the place is Fort Knox."

"I don't like the sound of this," Ginger said.

"I think I'll call the sheriff, and maybe even become self-destructive and call Tom in on it."

Ginger knew Taylor Jackson had a longtime competition going with Tom Bremer, the sheriff's deputy, and it was hard for Taylor to swallow his pride and ask for Tom's help. This must be bad.

"Please don't tell me you think this could be Sandi Jameson's killer," she said.

"That's who I'm thinking. Rick Fenrow has motive, and he has opportunity now that he's out of prison. His father most likely had money squirreled away all over the place, and Rick would have known where to find it."

"Thanks for that comforting assurance," she said with a sigh.

"You're welcome. I'm going to start making some calls and see if I can get to the bottom of this thing before I have to disturb you again."

"Let me give you Larry Bager's number. He's here with us. He needs to earn his keep." Ginger gave the number to Larry's room, hung up, then returned to bed and closed her eyes. It would be no good calling her brother at this time in the morning. Graham couldn't do anything about a break-in at Hideaway.

She was about to nod off when that abominable rooster crowed once more. It was one time too many.

Shoving her blanket aside again, she sprang from the bed, stalked to the sliding-glass door and slid it open to step out onto the lanai. "Stupid roosters."

Last night at the airport she'd thought they were so beautiful, wandering free around the grounds.

They weren't beautiful now, they were obnoxious. The gentleman at the front desk had explained that during a past hurricane the domesticated chickens had escaped from their pens, then had propagated. Profusely, it seemed.

Another crow disturbed her, and she glanced in the direction of the noise to see a shadow moving—not a chicken, but something much larger. She gasped, then scrambled back inside and grabbed up the receiver of the room phone.

Larry answered on the first ring. "What is it?" He sounded groggy and irritable.

"This is Ginger. Someone's lurking in the shadows outside."

The grogginess receded. "Where?"

"Below us in that little copse of palm trees."

"Could be security."

"Hiding in the shadows?" As soon as she spoke, there was a squawk and cackle. "The chickens are raising the alert. Don't you have your window open? Can't you hear that?"

"You have your *window* open? Ginger Carpenter, are you crazy? Use some common sense, woman!"

"I am. We're on the fourth floor. No one's getting to us from outside."

"You don't *know* what this man is capable of," Larry snapped.

"Why don't you go downstairs and make sure the lurker isn't up to something? The security might not be the tightest around here, and I especially doubt they're prepared for the likes of Rick. It isn't as if they have a lot of crime on this island."

"I'm on it. Close your window and make sure the other windows in your suite are shut and locked."

She did as she was told, then slipped quietly into the room Willow shared with the girls. She sank into the recliner, sure she wouldn't be able to sleep the rest of the night.

* * *

Ray herded the squawking chickens out onto the sand, then stood watching them for several minutes to make sure they kept going in the right direction. He'd been told last night when checking in that security kept close watch on the wandering fowl in this area, and that there was seldom a problem. This must be a fluke.

For a moment, tired as he was, Ray stared out at the rolling breakers and luxuriated in the feel of the salt air on his skin, the scent of it, the cool breeze on his face. Paradise. Enchantment.

Though he'd traveled to Hawaii twice before, those trips had been for continuing medical education conferences on Maui and Oahu. This trip was to celebrate the vows of two people in love.

It seemed to him as if he could feel the difference in the air on this island.

"Ray Clyde, you're a hopeless romantic fool," he muttered under his breath as he turned to walk back to his room. Hopeless was definitely the word. The difference in the air probably had something to do with the approaching storm.

A shadow moved to his left. A man stepped from beneath the eave of the building and came toward him. Fast.

Ray thought suddenly about Fenrow. Had that escaped con truly been able to follow and find them here in such a short time? Instinctively backing away, Ray reached into his pocket for his cell phone.

"Stop right there and put your hands where I can see them," the man said. "Now!"

Heart pounding as loudly as the waves, Ray did as he was told. The man marched across the grass, pistol in hand and at the ready. The familiarity of the voice registered, and Ray groaned.

"Larry, is that you?"

The man stopped.

"It's me, Larry. Ray Clyde. What are you doing out here in the middle of the night holding up strangers with a gun?"

Larry didn't redirect his pistol immediately, as if he wasn't convinced of Ray's authenticity. "What are *you* doing, lurking in the tree shadows below Willow's suite?"

"I wasn't lurking, I was chasing away a disturber of the peace."

The pistol lowered, and Larry stepped closer. "How long have you been down here?"

"Long enough to get the job done, why?"

"Were you beneath those trees over there?" Larry asked, pointing toward a stand of palm trees and poinciana.

"I wasn't even near there. I came around from the other side and ran full tilt at the roosters."

Larry stepped closer. "If that's so, then can you tell me why Ginger looked down from her lanai and saw someone standing there?"

"Did she say it was me?"

Larry hesitated. "No, but I hoped it was."

"Security, then?"

"I spoke with security before I came out here," Larry said. "There wasn't anyone in this area."

Ray cast a glance around them. "It wasn't me, Larry. Look, do you think we could continue this conversation on the way back upstairs? We could both use some beauty sleep. Morning's here, according to some psycho roosters."

Larry, too, cast a glance around. "Yeah. Could just be someone else got tired of the wake-up call." But he didn't sound convinced. He turned and led the way back to the building.

Ray followed, unable to resist one more glance into the surrounding shadows. Things had to get better than this. Today was a wedding day, after all. And this was Hawaii. Things like this weren't supposed to happen in paradise.

TWELVE

Far too early on Tuesday morning, Ginger met Willow in the small kitchenette of their suite with a cup of coffee. "This will get those eyes open. It's heavily leaded."

Willow accepted the cup with a smile. She looked well rested, which meant she hadn't been awakened by the early morning serenade of the chickens. "You've been up awhile?"

"Too long." Ginger took a too-large gulp from her own cup, then winced as the brew burned down her throat. "Today's the big day. If we're going to get some shopping done before we leave for the river, we'd better get started soon after breakfast."

Willow studied Ginger's face. "You know, we don't actually have to do any shopping this morning. You have your dress, and even though I think the girls would love new Hawaiian dresses for the wedding, it isn't totally necessary."

Ginger grimaced. "I look that bad?"

"You always look beautiful, but you don't look rested. Didn't sleep well last night?"

"I got a few hours before the chickens decided it was morning."

Willow chuckled. "I *thought* I heard a rooster crow, but decided I must have dreamed it."

"Did you hear anything else?" Ginger asked.

"Nope. I was pretty much dead to the world last night. I wouldn't have expected it, with all of today's excitement."

Ginger nodded, relieved. There would be time later to fill Willow in on the call from Taylor Jackson.

"I didn't get a chance to ask you last night because of the girls, but did you and Ray ever get things straightened out?" Willow asked.

"Not exactly, and I'm sure this won't be the time for it. This is your day."

"Yes, and hopeless romantic that I am," Willow said, giving Ginger a pointed look, "I would love to see everyone getting along and happy together."

"I'll be a perfect angel. Just keep Ray Clyde out of my gun sights." Ginger said it lightly, intending for Willow to take it as a joke.

Willow didn't laugh. She didn't even smile. With a quiet sigh, she set her coffee cup on the counter in the kitchenette and placed a hand on Ginger's arm. Her earnest eyes focused intently on Ginger. "You don't think the two of you will be able to work this thing out?"

Ginger was sorry she couldn't be more accommodating. "The problem didn't develop overnight—well, okay, to me it did seem to happen that way, even though I know Ray must have planned things without my knowledge for quite some time. But a decision that impacted my whole life? It'll take some time for me to come to terms with."

"I know I must sound like a nag," Willow said, retrieving her cup for another sip. "I only want to see you happy."

Ginger bit her tongue. She would not state the obvious—that she would be much happier if Ray was back in Missouri right now. Willow already knew that.

"I chose you to be my matron of honor because you have become like a sister to me," Willow said softly. "As a favor to me on this special day, would you please try one more time?"

Ginger scowled at her. "You know, I remember when you didn't hesitate to tell me when I was being too pushy or invasive in your life."

"That's right, but I'm learning some of your bad habits."

"Excuse me, but this habit came straight from Graham. Don't forget that."

"This is important to me."

"Fine," Ginger said, with as much graciousness as she could muster under the circumstances. "I'll do my best to play nice, but I'm only doing it for you."

Willow grinned and gave Ginger a quick, one-armed hug, careful to keep her coffee from spilling. "I know you don't believe this right now, but you'll be doing it for yourself, as well. Let's get the children up and go to breakfast."

The elegant hotel dining area had windows from ceiling to floor that offered an enchanting view of the ocean. Ray could happily sit here and sip his herbal tea all morning as he watched the roll of the waves, the kiss of morning sunlight on the palms, the brilliant display of flowers, both inside the building and out on the well-manicured grounds. The waves were huge this morning, and he couldn't help thinking about the storm. There were red flags along the beach, a warning not to swim in the ocean.

He didn't drag his gaze from the wild beauty until Graham joined him at the small table for two.

"You look like death" came Graham's cheery greeting.

Ray made a face. "Jet lag."

"And maybe the effects of some nighttime wandering?"

"Larry told you about our rooster chase last night?"

"He hadn't intended to, but I heard the crowing and got up."

"Don't tell me you saw someone lurking in the trees, too." Now that Ray noticed, Graham also looked tired.

"I didn't see anyone but you and Larry having an argument before you returned to the building," Graham said. "I asked him about it this morning, and he confessed about the phone call from Taylor Jackson in the early morning—something he apparently hadn't planned to tell me today."

Ray frowned and shook his head. "Taylor Jackson?"

"You mean he didn't tell you, either? Taylor's a local ranger who does extra time as a first responder in Hideaway, and sometimes helps out with law enforcement, since our town borders Mark Twain National Forest. Seems my house was invaded sometime after we left yesterday."

Ray set his cup down and leaned forward. "Any idea who that might have been?"

"Can you guess?"

"Rick Fenrow."

"Unfortunately. If it *was* him, and if he's managed to evade the authorities, he could arrive here at any time. In fact, considering the circumstances Larry described, Fenrow might already be here—and could have been here for hours."

"No wonder Larry pulled a gun on me," Ray said.

"Sorry about that. He tends to have quick responses."

Again, Ray thought about the figure Ginger told Larry she had seen in the shadows of the trees. "I don't suppose anyone has a photograph of this man, do they? Or could Larry pull up something on him from the police files? I need to be able to watch for him. We all do. The Courtneys should be alerted, as well."

Graham nodded, then rubbed his eyes. "Larry's assured me he's taking care of all that, so he'll have a photo for you." Graham's friendly, light brown eyes held traces of shadows beneath them. His sandy-brown hair was tousled, as if he'd run his fingers through it in frustration.

"I'll check with Larry as soon as he comes down for breakfast," Ray said. "If nothing else, I may be able to bring something up on the Internet."

Graham nodded, then his attention shifted to the entrance. "And here, at last, are the most important reasons for this trip."

Ray looked over his shoulder to see Willow strolling into the dining room with a child on either side of her. Tall and slender, with short, dark brown hair, Willow looked radiant, from the glow of her smiling eyes to the tilt of her firm chin.

Each child held a hand of their future mom as they walked into the dining room. Ray could see the love in the girls' faces. He especially saw the trust in Lucy's expression, and he was glad, knowing from observation that the precocious child trusted few people.

Ginger followed a few feet behind Willow and the girls, as if intentionally giving Willow and Graham exclusive time with the children. The newlyweds would be separated from the girls much of the time during the honeymoon, so they would want to lavish all the attention they could on Lucy and Brittany today.

Graham beckoned his fiancée to a table for four—the only one he could secure in the busy dining room. He then motioned Ginger toward Ray's table next to theirs.

Ray grimaced at the brief look of misgiving in Ginger's expression, but she recovered quickly, and actually smiled at him.

It looked to him as if that smile took too much effort, but perhaps he was being overly sensitive in his sleep-deprived state.

He rose and held the chair for her. "I hear the roosters disturbed you as badly as they did me last night."

She took the seat and nodded to the server offering coffee. "Don't tell me you slept with your windows open, too. Larry will get you for that."

"Larry almost shot me last night on the grounds."

She gave him a sheepish look of apology. "Sorry about that. It was my fault." She gave a suitable impression of inspecting him. "He obviously resisted the urge."

He nodded. "I can only hope he will continue his goodwill, at least until after the wedding today. I don't want anything to distract from the main focus of our trip."

She grinned. "Larry's pretty determined to keep us all safe."

Ray allowed himself to relax slightly. He loved Ginger's smile, especially when it was directed at him. "I hear the buffet is scrumptious. All kinds of exotic Hawaiian dishes along with typical breakfast fare."

"I've already checked it out," she said. "I'm going for the tropical waffle with bacon and mango. I want to see if they're anywhere as good as Bertie Meyer's black walnut waffles back home, which I doubt they are." She picked up her plate and went to the buffet table.

Ray smiled to himself. Maybe Ginger was as determined as he was to keep the peace this morning.

THIRTEEN

Ginger speared slices of pineapple and mango and laid them across her waffle. She accepted guava-citrus juice from the attendant at the breakfast bar, then glanced back at Ray. She should feel badly about sending Larry after him last night.

"Bacon?" asked another attendant.

Ginger nodded, smiling. Ray had always been able to hold his own in practically any situation. She doubted a simple confrontation with Larry would have concerned him, even if it had been at gunpoint.

When she joined him at the table, he greeted her with one of his dazzling smiles. Even in the morning light, after a night of little sleep, he might tend to look particularly appealing to some susceptible women. His dark hair, which looked as if he'd barely combed it, fell over his forehead rakishly.

He had always possessed that special ability to make anyone with him feel as if she were the most important person to him at the moment, that she had his full attention.

Nevertheless, appearances and actions could be deceiving. Honor mattered to her much more than physical appearance or an appealing personality. Character was of utmost importance.

She glanced at his breakfast selection, and wrinkled her nose. "Oatmeal and fruit? How unimaginative."

"Old habits die hard. Besides, this is authentic Hawaiian oatmeal and fruit, sweetened with authentic coconut milk."

No wonder he was in such good shape. She suddenly found herself reconsidering her own selections. If she wished to impress him with her good health and promise for a future in the mission field…

"I don't eat like this all the time," she said.

"Okay," he said, as if not sure why she would say that.

"In fact, I've lost thirty pounds since last April."

He nodded and took a sip of his tea. "That's good, Ginger, but you don't want to overdo it. You look great just as you are."

She patted her stomach for emphasis. "Cholesterol is down below two hundred, and my heart is as fit as Shoji Tabuchi's fiddle."

He raised an eyebrow.

"You know," she said, feeling silly all of a sudden, "Shoji? The famous violinist in Branson?"

"You're starting again," he said.

"Starting what?"

"Your campaign for Belarus."

She leaned back in her seat. "That's ridiculous. Just because I don't feel ready to be put out to pasture—"

"You were never put out to pasture, Ginger."

"After all the trouble I've gone to with my weight loss

program and exercise, if my health ever really had anything at all to do with my banishment, I feel I should at least be given another chance to serve in—"

"I think today should be about Graham and Willow's wedding."

She heard the warning in his voice. She couldn't help herself. "Of course it is, and one reason I'm open to discussion is because Willow specifically asked me to try one more time to reach some kind of understanding with you so we would be able to cooperate as a team today. I'm simply responding to her request."

His dark blue eyes filled with affectionate humor.

"Don't laugh at me," she warned, picking up her fork. No one could accuse her of allowing an argument to kill her appetite. Besides, all this contact with Ray was beginning to affect her in a strange way. It made her long for those times when they were friends. Or, at least, when she thought they were friends.

"I'd never do that," he said softly. "However, I can't help being impressed by your tenacity."

"Thank you. This tenacity works well on the mission field, as well." She bit into a piece of mango, and savored its sweetness, expecting him to smile at her jibe at least.

He didn't smile. He leaned forward, holding her gaze. "Ginger, you were right last night. Your health wasn't the only reason I pulled you out of the country."

She paused, studying his expression. He looked sad.

No, sad wasn't the word. He looked remorseful. She'd spent quite some time before sleep trying to figure out exactly what he'd been talking about.

"But it was one of the reasons," she said. "You told me that."

"Yes, it was. Graham and I were both concerned by the sudden appearance of your heart abnormality."

"It was nothing, just stress." She took a bite of the waffle. Wonderful. Maybe not quite as good as Bertie's, though.

"That's exactly my point," he said. "What was causing that stress?"

She shrugged. "The same kind of thing that causes stress in any job, on our own soil or in foreign lands. There will always be difficulties and interpersonal conflicts."

"But we can't afford interpersonal conflicts on foreign soil, Ginger. We're ambassadors to Belarus, to every country on which our representatives set foot."

"That's ridiculous. It isn't possible to interact with others on a daily basis and avoid conflict at all times."

He looked down into his cup, as if seeking an answer there.

This time she did put her fork down. "Ray, are you saying someone on my staff complained about me?" But that was ridiculous. In spite of occasional conflicts, she had been close to her whole staff, both American and Belarusian.

"Your staff loved you," he said. "The comments that concerned me were not from them."

"Comments? Now we're getting somewhere." And she suddenly wondered if she wanted to find out where this conversation was headed. "Who were they from?"

He took a sip of tea, set the cup down and leaned back. "It's something I've put off talking to you about because…well…anyway, I think it's time we talked about it. Not this morning, though. I don't want anything to place any more of a pall on this day."

Ginger swallowed hard, resisting the urge to press the discussion. She wanted to know what he was referring to. *Needed* to know. But she also needed to create a favorable impression on him, for once, not force his hand as she had done last year.

Yes, she knew she'd done it. She'd forced him to choose between her and her replacement. That incident hadn't ended well.

He dipped his spoon into the oatmeal, and she followed his lead by picking up her fork again. The food was fabulous. Fresh fruit, ripened on the vine, certainly added a lot of flavor…as did the pure butter and crispy crunch of the waffle that probably packed a wallop of calories that should last her all day. If only they would…

Ray sighed and looked at her again. "As an aside, the clinic was growing, Ginger. It needed a licensed medical trainer who could oversee the Belarusian medical residents' training through the clinic, so they would be prepared to take over the management of operations in case we were ousted from the program." He paused, then added quietly. "Or in case we decided to terminate it ourselves."

"That's ridiculous. You would never do that." She took another bite of the waffle, savored it slowly. *Keep your mouth shut, Ginger. Don't press the subject. Smile and agree with him. Don't put him in argument mode, because you know Ray Clyde in argument mode is not where you want him to be.*

"So you're saying you expect Belarus to close their borders to medical missionaries sometime soon?" she asked, merely as a way to extend a polite conversation.

He paused with another spoonful of oatmeal halfway to his mouth, and closed his eyes.

She frowned at him. "Ray? There's no chance of that, is there?"

"Not imminently, no, but in case they do, we need to be ready with nationals to take over. The clinics are important, and you yourself encountered the fierce national pride those people have." He swallowed, cleared his throat. "They need to feel that they're being honored in their professions, not looked down upon as second-class professionals."

"Of course," she said. "You're absolutely right." He couldn't possibly be accusing her of treating the Belarusians—on whom she had lavished so much love—like second-class citizens.

"I'm not accusing you of anything, Ginger."

She felt a trickle of deepening anxiety. Had she spoken her thoughts aloud? To her amazement, she did lose her appetite.

"I know that look," he said. "I've seen it often enough." He put his spoon down. "Ginger, I'm simply telling you what kind of a spot I was in last year. I needed something you couldn't provide. I needed what amounted to a residency trainer. A doctor."

She held his gaze. If the real reason he'd pulled her out of Belarus was because he needed a trainer to take her place, he'd have told her that last year.

"Even so, you could have brought someone in and

kept me there to help out," she said. "I didn't have to be the director, I just needed to be there. I still do. I could help whoever is there."

"And I'm telling you that it isn't a possibility at this point."

She dropped her fork to the table, aware that the clatter caused several to look her direction. "So this *is* personal."

He seemed to have lost his appetite, as well. His moment of hesitation sealed the fate of this conversation.

"I think I could use some fresh air." She rose from the table, feeling the rejection as a fresh wound, as painful as it had been last year. He wasn't talking about someone else's complaint, he was talking about his own.

"Ginger, you're jumping to the wrong—"

"Oh, stop it." It was difficult to keep her voice down. "Drop the subject, okay? I'm taking a quick walk on the beach before everyone leaves to go shopping."

"I don't think you should—"

She fixed him a look of warning. "If I want to walk on the beach instead of sharing a meal with someone who has no respect for my medical or interpersonal skills, then I—"

"That's the most ridiculous thing you've said yet," he snapped. "I told you we'd talk about it later."

She looked around at the others, and found Graham and Willow watching them. "Keep your voice down. Better yet, return to your oatmeal. I've got a beach to check out."

He stood up, obviously determined to follow her. The man sometimes had the social skills of one of those obnoxious bantam roosters out in the yard.

"If you really want to keep peace on this trip, then you'll give me some space right now," she warned, then turned and marched from the room. She stopped at the door, unable to resist a glance back.

He tossed his napkin onto the table, took a final swallow of tea and caught up with her. "I feel like a walk, myself," he said as he joined her at the door.

"Then you *don't* want to keep the peace?" she muttered.

"I happen to think there are some things more important," he said, staying a step behind her. "I also believe you will stop somewhere short of murder on Graham and Willow's wedding day, especially with the children looking on."

"Don't try to shame me. It's Graham and Willow who should be ashamed for pulling this nightmare of a trip on me without any warning, as if I don't have a mind of my own." She knew she was repeating herself, but the truth bore repeating.

"You're saying I'm the nightmare?" Ray asked.

She looked over her shoulder at him, and she could have sworn that comment had hurt his feelings. Amazing. Why should he be surprised?

"Take it however you wish to take it," she muttered. "Now, would you please leave me alone?"

"Your medical skills are excellent, and your ability to deal with patients is unequaled. That's never been a problem, and I resent your implication that I ever said it was."

She blinked at him. "Good, then I should receive an excellent recommendation from you next time one is requested, right?"

"That all depends on—"

"Good, I'm glad we agree," she said. "I have contacts with other agencies. Now will you please leave me alone? I need a chance to lick my wounds in private."

He followed. "How could I have wounded you? All I did was tell you that you have the best medical skills, as well as patient skills. What's to take offense about that?"

"You implied that this vendetta you have against me is personal," she said. "Obviously, you have your reasons for not trusting me in a management position at one of the clinics."

"Your words, not mine. My concern is the same as it's always been—your safety. And if it seems that I take your welfare a little too personally, well, sue me for caring enough to speak my mind."

She turned and looked up at him, well aware that they stood within sight of the others inside the dining room— others who could be watching. She needed to start setting a better example for the children.

So she smiled. After his initial surprise, Ray smiled back, though his expression was tentative, as if he didn't trust her seeming capitulation.

In that moment, she realized that, in spite of everything, she was not immune to the apparent sincerity in Ray Clyde's eyes, or to the nearness of his broad shoulders. The intensity of his focus—fixed on her at the moment—was working just the way she was sure he'd intended.

How could a man like Ray, with the intellect, passion

and focus of a genius, have that special way about him that made a woman want to know him better?

And how was it that she suddenly felt more alive than she had since she'd last seen him? Yes, she was still angry. But that emotion suddenly seemed preferable to the frustration she'd felt for so many months.

In spite of her anger, she suddenly felt...hope?

"Keep in mind," he said, "that as medical director of GlobeMed, I would be asked to recommend you for any other organization to which you would apply, just like last time. I'm still concerned for your health."

"You're saying you wouldn't give me a good recommendation to return?"

"Not to Minsk. Not to Belarus."

She clenched her teeth, leaning toward him. "How about deepest, darkest Africa?"

"Not at this time. But, you know, I would have placed you elsewhere last year had there been an opening. And if you will remember, I did offer you a job in Columbia."

"Working at your clinic."

"Would that have been so bad?"

"That was nothing more than an attempt to appease me."

His eyes narrowed. "I don't think you're qualified to analyze my motives, since you tend to hold everything I say or do suspect."

She turned and marched toward the roaring waves. Several times after she'd returned home last year, Ray had attempted to contact her, either through Graham, or by calling her on her cell phone. He'd even resorted to writing a few letters, cards of apology, notes of entreaty, and when she didn't reply, he had finally come to see her. She'd told him to stay away.

She had to ask herself now, why had he tried so hard to make amends last year if he truly hadn't cared?

FOURTEEN

Ray watched Ginger try to make a dignified retreat while stepping onto the sand in her flip-flops. She finally stopped and pulled them off to go barefoot. Now that she'd mentioned it, he noticed she truly had lost some weight since he'd last seen her. She looked great.

Ginger Carpenter was a woman whose beauty was secondary to her personality. Not that she wasn't beautiful—she was to him. But her strength and outspoken charm was most striking at first meeting. The combined attractiveness of her antique copper hair, freckles, warm brown eyes and that indefinable inner glow—though sometimes it was the glow of hot anger—wasn't easily forgotten.

Ray had never even tried.

Surprisingly, her response to him today had encouraged him. A heated battle with Ginger was much preferable to being frozen out of her life, as he had been since last March. Sure, today she'd been trying to persuade him to allow her back on the mission field, but at least she was talking to him.

He watched as she ran into the waves up to her knees,

splashing with the abandon of a child. How he would have loved, years ago, to be a part of her life. But she had made it obvious that she didn't believe romance would ever be a possibility for her again. She saw herself as old at fifty-three.

She had been married and divorced, then married and widowed. She had two grown sons from her first marriage, and lots of good memories from her second. Her boys were healthy and well-adjusted and living in Missouri; one in Kansas City and one in St. Louis. Both married, both without children yet, though Ginger was hopeful.

Ray smiled when a wave caught Ginger by surprise and nearly knocked her off her feet.

"Now there's a lady who knows how to have fun and make a fool of herself at the same time" came a voice from behind Ray.

He glanced around to see Larry Bager, dressed in the white slacks and red and blue Hawaiian shirt, which Willow had decided would be the uniform of the day for the men in the wedding party. The concierge had delivered the shirts earlier this morning from Hilo Hattie's in Lihue.

Ray didn't see any evidence of Larry's gun this morning. "Have you had breakfast?"

"Not yet. Graham told me you and Preston will be available to watch over the kids all day today."

"Of course. Let me know what you need. It would help if I knew what Rick Fenrow looked like."

Larry pulled a folded sheet of paper from his shirt pocket, unfolded it and handed it to Ray. "That's pretty recent, but don't count on the exact appearance. I expect the black hair and bushy black eyebrows to be changed, but he sure can't fix that ski-ramp nose or those thin lips."

"He could've grown a mustache," Ray said. "That could change a lot of things."

Larry grunted his agreement. "And his eye color could be altered with contact lenses."

Larry nodded his head toward Ginger, who walked along the edge of the water, head down, sandals dangling from her hand. "Tell her next time she wants me to help you chase chickens, she needs to tell me, and not scare me to death with some story about a man lurking in the shadows."

"She could have seen someone."

Larry stared after her for another few seconds. "I spoke with the girl at the front desk, and there was a call in the early morning hours from a florist shop asking for the room number of Willow Traynor."

"A florist shop from where?" Ray asked.

"A legitimate one from here in Poipu. When the clerk told the caller that the bellman would deliver the flowers to the room once they arrived at the hotel, the caller disconnected. No flowers are yet in evidence. Since the hotel office has caller ID, and since they did see the number for that particular florist shop, I'm still trying to find out what's going on with that. There could be a legitimate mistake somewhere along the line."

"Whose names were registered last night when we checked in?" Ray asked. "Steve and Helen handled all of that."

"Helen has assured me that she and Steve registered under their own names due to the increased safety concerns."

"But Rick Fenrow would already know where we're staying because of the information he would have found at Graham's house," Ray said. "I doubt he'll stop at a simple telephone call, if that was him."

Larry shook his head. "Fenrow's proven in the past that he's willing to go to any lengths for his revenge. I've already spoken with hotel security and the local police. I've made sure everyone has a photograph faxed to their offices."

"I'll do all I can to help. In fact," Ray said, nodding toward the slight bulge he finally detected beneath Larry's shirt, "I'd be more than happy to pack some heat, myself."

Larry eyed him with interest. "You know how to shoot?"

"I've carried a weapon for protection from time to time in my line of work."

"I heard you were a pediatrician," Larry said, obviously not impressed.

"Among other things. I know how to handle a pistol. Got one for me?"

"No, but I can get one if I feel it's warranted. I'll let you know."

"Graham can handle a pistol, too," Ray said.

"Yes, but it's Graham's wedding day. No man should have to worry about this kind of thing on the day he's losing his freedom."

"He needs to be able to protect himself and his family."

Larry nodded. "That's what I'm here for."

"Did you get a weather report last night?"

"Sure did. We may see a storm by tonight, but aside from some rough waters and hefty winds, we should be okay for the wedding." Larry glanced once more toward Ginger on the beach, then back at Ray. "Now, if we can keep any other kinds of storms from breaking out today, we should be set."

Lucy smashed her waffle with her fork and placed a small bite in her mouth. It tasted good, but she wasn't hungry. How could she eat when there were so many things to see? Especially since she and Brittany popped a bag of popcorn in the microwave in their room as soon as they got up this morning. It woke up poor Aunt Ginger, but she didn't yell at them.

"There are my two special little girls!" came a voice from behind Lucy, and she turned to see Helen Courtney pulling an empty chair from the next table.

The lady placed two huge gift bags on the floor, one beside Lucy's chair, and one beside Brittany's, then sat down and gave them another big smile.

The bag beside Brittany was pink, her favorite color. Lucy's was red. How did Helen know?

"Want to see your present?" Helen asked, nudging the red gift bag closer to Lucy. "I picked it out especially for you. Go ahead, open it and see what I got you."

Lucy loved presents. She'd gotten more of those since moving in with Graham and Aunt Ginger than she'd ever even seen when Mama was alive. But she wasn't sure of this one. She eyed the shiny red bag. It wasn't as big as Brittany's bag.

"What's in it?"

Helen laughed. "You're supposed to open it and see."

Lucy watched Brittany pull a beautiful white stuffed bear out of her pink bag. Her eyes widened, and she clapped her hands. "A friend for Chuckles!"

Lucy wasn't impressed. What could a little kid do with a white bear besides get it dirty?

"Maybe they're cousins," Helen suggested. "Anyway, he's all nice and clean and huggable. I thought maybe you'd like to give Mr. Chuckles a little bit of a rest, and make friends with this bear instead. You can give him a name, comb his hair, and meanwhile I'll give Mr. Chuckles a bath."

Brittany's smile died. "But Mr. Chuckles is a bear, silly. Bears don't take baths. Don't you know that?"

Lucy reached into her red bag and pulled out a huge piece of green cloth with bright pink, purple and blue flowers.

"That's a wrap for your swimsuit, sweetheart," Helen said. "You can use it as a cover-up when we go to the beach. You'll look like a beautiful Hawaiian princess."

Lucy touched the cloth and held it against her cheek. It felt soft, and it looked like Hawaii's flowers.

Helen smiled, her face filling with wrinkles. Lucy liked her.

"Now," Helen said, turning back to Brittany. "I know a bear doesn't have to take a bath when he lives in the forest, because he gets a bath whenever it rains." Helen reached for the toy in question. "But Chuckles doesn't have that option. Why don't we give him a nice, cool wash in the hotel washing machine so he won't feel out of place with the rest of us washed bears."

Brittany's mouth flew open, and she grabbed Chuckles out of Helen's hands. "No! We can't ever wash him, Mama said so. You leave him alone!"

"Brittany," Willow warned. "That's no way to behave with someone who is giving you a gift. Haven't we discussed how important it is to be polite?"

Brittany only held Chuckles tighter. "Mama said we must never wash him, must never let anyone else have him, must take good care of him."

"I know, but Helen went to a lot of trouble to pick out this special present for you, and she's treated you with nothing but kindness. Now thank her."

Brittany set her lips and jutted out her chin, and she glared at Helen. "I don't want some stupid white bear."

"Brittany!" Lucy shouted. "Don't be such a brat!"

Brittany ignored her. "Chuckles is mine, and you can't have him!" She slid from her chair and ran from the room.

Willow got up and rushed after her.

Lucy felt her face turn hot.

"Oh, I'm so sorry," Helen said. "I was so worried about germs, you see, and especially after a long flight, that I thought—"

"You have nothing to apologize for," Graham assured her. "We'll need to work with Brittany a little about her manners."

Lucy cringed. Why did her little sister have to be a brat at the worst times?

Helen left the table, and had just reached the door when Lucy caught her breath. She hadn't even thanked Helen for the present.

While Graham returned to the buffet table for

seconds, and Willow knelt outside the double glass doors talking to Brittany, Lucy scooted from her chair. She ran after Helen, following her outside into a stone-paved garden that overlooked the ocean. There were chairs and tables set up here, and Helen joined her husband at a table.

"I'll never forgive Sandi for what she did to those little girls," Helen said, her voice sharp as she sank down beside Steve.

Lucy stopped at the mention of her mother's name. Neither Helen nor Steve saw her, as they sat facing the ocean.

"You don't have a choice now," Steve said. "She's dead."

Helen picked up her milk and took a sip. "It didn't have to be that way."

"Lucy!" came Graham's frantic voice from the doorway.

Steve and Helen turned as Graham rushed to Lucy and took her arm. "Sweetheart, you need to let us know where you are at all times. Don't go running off like that. You gave us a scare."

Lucy met Helen's gaze, saw her eyes widen, and her lips part, then Helen exchanged glances with Steve.

"I—I'm sorry," Lucy murmured to Graham. "I wanted to thank Helen for the present. I thought since I was with Helen, I'd be...safe."

Before Helen could respond, Lucy tugged on Graham's hand and pulled him back inside. Why were they talking about Mama like they knew her?

FIFTEEN

On Tuesday afternoon, Lucy stood beside a railing of the large boat—they called it a pontoon—and held tightly to her sister's hand. Branches and vines, green and grasping, seemed to reach toward them from the shore as their boat chugged up the Wailua River toward the Fern Grotto.

"Sissy, stop it. You're hurting me!" Brittany tried to pull away.

Lucy wouldn't let her go. "Then hold on to the rail."

"Ouch!"

Aunt Ginger shot Lucy a warning look over her shoulder. "It's okay, Lucy. You can relax."

Pressing her lips into a tight line, Lucy released Brittany's hand only to grab her by the shoulders.

Brittany tried to shrug her off. "Let me go!"

"Stop whining," Lucy whispered. "People will think you're a little brat." Which she was. But sometimes the warning worked because Brittany liked people to like her.

Most of the time it didn't work.

Aunt Ginger finally turned and leaned toward Lucy,

took her hands and made her let go of Brittany. "I said you could relax." She smelled good, like the flower in her hair.

Lucy resisted the urge to grab Brittany again. "Why are you wearing your flower at the back of your head instead of over your ear, Aunt Ginger? The lady at the store told me a single woman's supposed to wear her flower over the—"

"Sweetheart, I don't think anyone cares whether or not I'm married. Besides, I don't want anyone to think I'm some desperate female looking for a man, because I'm not."

"Okay." Lucy sighed.

"Lucy, remember what we talked about last night?" Aunt Ginger could be firm when she wanted to. Not mean, just firm. Like today.

Lucy nodded. They'd talked about a lot of things after lights-out, when Aunt Ginger and Willow, Lucy and Brittany had sat listening to the waves through the screen on the window. It had been fun—what Lucy always thought a girls' sleepover would be like—not that she'd ever been to one.

So why was Aunt Ginger so cranky now?

"You're supposed to be a little calmer with your sister," Aunt Ginger said.

Oh. That's the talk she meant. Lucy sighed.

"You don't need to be her bodyguard every single second. You need to enjoy this day, and let her enjoy it, too."

Lucy looked at Brittany, who stuck out her tongue. What if Brittany fell into the water? They wore bright, flowery dresses, and they had flowers in their hair. The dresses wouldn't look pretty all wet from the river. And what if a crocodile ate Brittany before she could be saved?

Helen had told Lucy that there weren't any crocodiles in Hawaii, but Uncle Preston didn't think Helen knew much. What if she didn't know about crocodiles?

Helen knew about Mama, though. That was something Lucy couldn't forget. How did Helen and Steve know Mama?

Aunt Ginger put an arm around Lucy's shoulders. "We'll be passing a traditional Hawaiian village in a few minutes."

"Are we going to stop and look at it?" Lucy asked.

"No. It seems we only have the boat for two and a half hours, and so we have to do the exchange of vows and get back down the river." She shook her head and muttered, "Not exactly the romantic upriver cruise we'd expected, but we've got to get back in time for the luau, anyway."

"What's that?" Lucy asked. "Nobody ever told me."

"It's when they roast a pig in the ground, and then dig it up and eat it with poi."

"Eww. What's poi?"

Aunt Ginger chuckled at the look on Lucy's face. "It's taro root, honey. You know, for Hawaiians, it's the same as potatoes are for us."

"So a luau is a dinner of dirty, burned pork and potatoes?" Lucy shook her head. It didn't take much to make grown-ups happy, did it?

"They also have a show of the traditional dances and stories of the history of Hawaii."

Lucy frowned. "A history lesson, too?"

"Boring," Brittany said.

"I don't think you'll be bored," Aunt Ginger assured them both.

Lucy sighed. She couldn't wait until they could go swim at the beach. But would it be safe? If there could be alligators or crocodiles in this river, couldn't they also swim out to the beach? And what if Steve and Helen knew about them, and were lying because they wanted—

Aunt Ginger chuckled again, and Lucy looked up and met her gaze.

· With a warm smile, Aunt Ginger bent over and kissed Lucy on the forehead, then rubbed at the spot to wipe away the lipstick. Aunt Ginger hardly ever wore lipstick.

"Sweetheart, I can see that mind of yours traveling a million miles an hour. What are you thinking about right now?"

"Crocodiles." *And Helen and Steve.*

Aunt Ginger laughed out loud.

"Don't make fun of me," Lucy said. But she wasn't mad. She loved hearing Aunt Ginger laugh, especially about crocodiles. If it was something to laugh about, then she knew she didn't have to worry.

"I'll try not to, but there are no crocodiles in these waters."

"That man at the dock said it was only a matter of time before someone sneaked a pet crocodile or alligator into Hawaii and set it loose. That would be horrible."

"It would, yes, but that's one more thing you don't have to worry about today." Aunt Ginger drew Lucy forward to join her at the railing of the boat. "You need to trust your sister a little more. She isn't going to jump overboard and get eaten by a crocodile."

Lucy turned and looked at Steve and Helen, who stood on the other side of the boat. And they were watching her. Again.

Ray couldn't help eavesdropping on the conversation taking place behind him. Though he dared not glance over his shoulder at Ginger and her young charges, he couldn't help chuckling to himself.

Until a few weeks ago, he hadn't dreamed he would be out here in the middle of Wailua River, wearing a bright Hawaiian shirt and white slacks, dressed as best man for the wedding of one of his dearest friends.

And he hadn't dreamed that the woman about whom he cared so much would have actually bid him a civil good morning. True, the ambience had deteriorated from there, and her courtesy had been in response to Willow's request, but at least Ginger had tried.

Maybe that meant she would try again, even if it was an act.

Her behavior with the children, however, was not an act. Having eavesdropped shamelessly on her conversation with Lucy and Brittany at the dock while waiting for the boat, Ray had drawn several conclusions.

First, of course, was the fact that Ginger still adored kids, and she needed a job that would enable her to interact with them. Nothing new there, of course.

Second, the interactions between Lucy and Brittany were characteristic of what he'd seen in other siblings who had endured a traumatic loss. Lucy mothered Brittany, and in so doing, encouraged Brittany to revert to the behavior of a much younger child at times.

Third, Ginger countered Lucy's attempts with a little overmothering, herself. Not that Ray would dare call her on it. At least, not at this point.

Interesting that he was presently in need of a physician's assistant in his office practice back home. Since children were his specialty, it seemed the opportunity to hire Ginger for that position would be a slam dunk.

It would be for anyone else, but he had approached that topic with her last year, and had been soundly put in his place. That subject would need to be approached next time with great diplomacy.

Though he did believe in miracles, and had actually witnessed a few in his lifetime, he had serious doubts about that happening in this situation.

Why should God break protocol and perform a miracle for the man who had been so hard on Ginger and flubbed the whole situation?

He turned away from the others impatiently and stood watching the boat's wake on the surface of the river. Why was he suddenly second-guessing his decisions last year? Ginger's response to his presence was affecting him. Ridiculous to allow one person to cause him to doubt himself and his own motivations. He knew better.

"Not motion sick, are you?" came a gruff voice from behind. He turned to see Larry Bager bracing himself against the railing of the boat. His vivid shirt hung loosely enough that no bulge showed from the holster and gun beneath—unless one knew he was carrying.

"I've never had that problem," Ray said. "You?"

"I hate the water."

"And yet you live in Branson, the Tri-Lakes Area?" Now that he mentioned it, Larry did look slightly pale.

"I never get near a boat if I can help it."

Ray grinned. "I'd live on one if it were possible. The rocking rhythm of the water eases the stresses of the day and can put me to sleep faster than warm milk and a sleeping pill."

"I don't suppose, then, that you would happen to be carrying a seasick tablet with you," Larry said.

"As a matter of fact, I have a small bottle in my pocket."

Larry brightened. "You take this doctoring thing seriously, don't you?"

Ray reached for the bottle. "I think it's the best man's responsibility, isn't it? To make sure the wedding guests don't get motion sick before the vows can be made?" He flipped the top and shook two tablets into Larry's hand. "Have you discovered more information about the call from the florist shop?"

Larry glanced over his shoulder, studied some people standing on the shore, then apparently dismissed them as harmless. "The policeman I spoke with said the florist doesn't keep money in his shop overnight, so he doesn't bother with a lot of security. Who'd want to rob a florist?"

"So even a schoolkid could have broken in without leaving evidence of entry," Ray said.

Larry nodded. "That's right. A call was made from the shop late last night. The florist swears he wasn't there, and made no such call."

"Fenrow is on the island."

"I called hotel security and asked that someone there pack all our luggage. That will be transported to a house near Haena State Park in the northern tip of the island. Very safe, and there's no way Fenrow could find us there."

Something in Ray relaxed. Larry did have things in hand.

"I also instructed the hotel staff to spread the word that if anyone called or appeared in person asking about us, we had left the island and were flying to Maui."

Ray nodded in approval. "Think the ruse will work?"

"Sure do. This man's not getting anywhere near our group."

"It won't hurt to remain vigilant," Ray said.

"Never hurts to do that."

"Do the others know we won't be returning to Poipu?" Ray asked.

Larry shook his head. "Let's enjoy the wedding if we can before we upset the apple cart. Know what I mean? I'll tell Steve and Helen about it afterward."

"What about the luau?"

"Sorry, can't do it. We'll have to change our whole itinerary. Anything that scum could've found in Graham's house, we need to delete from the list of things to do on this trip."

Ray grimaced. At least Lucy would be relieved about the luau. She didn't sound excited about the proposition, anyway. But she didn't know what she was missing. Ray had seen two of them, and had enjoyed them both.

"You know," Ray said to Larry, "those tablets could make you a little groggy. You don't think they'll affect your aim if you have to shoot, do you?"

Larry shot him a dark look of warning. "Keep your voice down."

"Sorry."

"And no, the drug won't affect me. I only hope I don't have to use my trigger finger for anything more than scratching my nose on this trip."

"I hope not, either."

"But I learned last year not to underestimate that man," Larry said. "He's surprised us before, but it's not gonna happen to me this time."

Ray nodded and wandered away. He only hoped Larry was right, but as sharp as the P.I. was, no one could be on patrol every second of the day. He had to sleep, had to have downtime.

Ray, too, was beginning to beware of strangers who stood too near the children or Willow. He'd do all he could to back up Larry.

A man would have to be desperate for revenge to attempt anything with this group.

Lucy kept her hands to herself, but she watched Larry Bager. Every time he glanced toward the shoreline, Lucy followed his gaze. Every time he studied the people on another boat, Lucy did so, as well.

He had a way of watching people, his gaze sliding toward them and away before they noticed.

Larry wasn't the kind of person to snuggle little kids on his lap and read them a story. He didn't smile like Ray did. Even though Aunt Ginger seemed to get along better with him than she did with Ray, Larry didn't smile much at Aunt Ginger, either.

When Lucy asked about it, Aunt Ginger explained that some men felt threatened by strong women. But Aunt Ginger didn't arm wrestle Larry or pick him up and carry him around, so he couldn't know how strong she was.

None of that mattered, though. Lucy didn't care if he never said a word or smiled at any of them, as long as he protected them. And maybe that was why he didn't talk. He wanted to be on guard all the time.

Another boat drew near theirs, and Lucy studied the tourists on board it. One man, standing near the back of the group of brightly dressed people, had black hair and wore sunglasses.

When Larry turned to look at him, Lucy hurried to Brittany's side and grabbed her hand. Let her whine.

SIXTEEN

Lucy once again grabbed her little sister. Brittany squirmed and tried to shove her away.

Ginger was about to intervene when she noticed Larry stiffening. His right hand raised almost imperceptibly to the hem of his shirt. His dark gaze fixed on someone in the crowded pontoon that was passing their boat on the left.

She followed the direction of his gaze, and saw a dark-haired man, pale face, slump shouldered, hanging away from the rest of the crowd. She tensed.

Willow stepped to Larry's side and nudged him, shaking her head. His hand lowered, and he relaxed. She sank to her knees beside the girls and spoke softly to them, an elegantly dressed bride more concerned about reassuring the children than preserving her appearance for the ceremony.

Ginger glanced again at the man in the other boat who resembled Rick Fenrow. It wasn't him, of course. No one would know that as surely as Willow, herself, who had stared into her abductor's face as he tried to kill her.

Someone stepped to the railing beside Ginger and

nudged her with an elbow. She glanced up to find Preston watching her, his blue-gray eyes filled with... what? Concern?

"You look tired," he said.

"Thanks."

"And a little sad."

"I thought your degree was in accounting, not counseling."

"I didn't say I wanted you to talk to me about it, I thought you might want to smile to make the bride and groom more comfortable."

"Can it wait until they're watching?" Ginger grumbled. "My face is tired. All of me is tired. I need sleep."

"And you need to get away from Ray Clyde," Preston guessed.

Ginger frowned at him. "You're meddling."

He shrugged. "That's my sister's job. And yours, most of the time."

Her frown deepened.

"It isn't my area of expertise," he said, "but why do you feel that you have to be on foreign soil in order to fulfill some sort of mission?"

"You sound like Ray now. Who said I needed foreign soil?"

"Isn't that what this whole thing with Ray is about? You're mad at him because he ruined your career in foreign missions?"

Ginger bit back a sharp reply about people minding their own business. She should be glad Preston was seeking answers to subjects that touched on the spiritual. She wished he'd do it at a more appropriate time—

like when she'd had some sleep and was prepared with better replies.

But, of course, her own well-planned replies didn't always have the desired effect. It seemed that she was most effective when she was too tired to think straight, and the Holy Spirit had a chance to take over her tongue.

"I've never known you to hold this kind of a grudge," Preston continued. "Especially with someone like Ray, who anybody can tell is a good-hearted person."

Hold on to the temper, Ginger. "Of course he has a good heart," she said. *To anyone but me.* "I'm afraid I'm not at my best right now. I'd love nothing better than a nice, long nap in a quiet room. If I seem to be brooding about something, I apologize." She forced a sweet smile and hoped he'd wander away to study the luxuriant foliage along the shore at the historical Hawaiian village.

Instead, he frowned and leaned against the railing. "I've always had trouble understanding the concept of Christian medical missions that manipulate the needs of patients in order to sell them Jesus."

Oh, brother, here it comes. Preston was in the mood to argue today. Why was that? And why couldn't he choose someone else?

"How do you see us manipulating, Preston? Meeting their physical needs gives us the opportunity to meet other needs they might not be so aware of, but we don't force anything on them."

"You're talking about spiritual needs," he said drily.

"We're not just physical beings—we're spiritual, and we have minds. But I don't have to tell you that. You grew up in a Christian home, you know—"

"It didn't take." His voice was flat, not angry, not frustrated, but matter-of-fact. "My prayers weren't answered. My mother remains schizophrenic to this day."

Ah. That was it. His and Willow's parents couldn't make it to the wedding because of their mother's most recent episode. Ginger knew, from long conversations with Willow, that Preston and Willow's mother's mental illness had influenced their lives profoundly.

"I know," she said. "I'm sorry. I'm not going to feed you the usual dogma about the mystery of God and why He does certain things. I'm sure you heard that for most of your childhood."

Preston rested his elbows against the railing as he stared down into the dark blue-green water. "Until I grew sick of hearing it and started asking questions. Then that got me into trouble, too. How *dare* I question God?"

"I understand," she said. "I've been there. I got so tired of those well-intentioned believers who tried to frighten me into believing what they did."

He nodded.

"Some people don't realize that others can't be bullied into sudden faith in Christ. It didn't work that way for me."

"Oh, no," Preston groaned. "You're getting ready to 'give me your testimony.'"

"You know what? You're the one who started this conversation."

He raised his hands in surrender. "Sorry. Go ahead and hit me with your best shot."

"All I'm saying is that, after I resisted the efforts of highly dogmatic people who tried hard to make me repent for huge past mistakes, I was touched by the gentle, loving voice of a dying woman in the hospital where my second husband died so many years ago. She simply told me to imagine that there was more to us than this present lifetime. That there was actually a much better life, and that Jesus had left directions for us to arrive there safely."

Preston looked at her, as if expecting something more profound. "That's it? That touched you?"

"I realized later that it wasn't her voice alone that led me to finally believe, but it was a combination of many voices over the years. Even those who seemed obnoxious, or nervous, or awkward. I realized that a lot of people cared enough about me to tell me something I didn't want to hear. God spoke to me through each of them. To me, that one dying patient had the quiet voice of God, a culmination of His love. His mercy. His peace."

That was the voice she wanted to be to others who so desperately needed that touch that could only come from the tender presence of the Holy Spirit. If only Preston could see that side of God.

But she wasn't doing such a good job of showing it to him. She, too, had been angry and judgmental on this trip. Actually, she'd been that way since last year. With Ray.

"You saw God in a dying patient," Preston said drily.

She sighed. Why even bother? How could he see anything of Christ's spirit through her own arrogance?

She closed her eyes, suddenly ashamed. *Oh, Lord, that's what I'm doing, isn't it? I'm so arrogant in my anger toward Ray, and it's also toward You.*

"Unfortunately," she said, "I've never quite outgrown

my early years of rebellion. Kind of hard to see the gentle love of Christ in me most of the time."

"In a way, I'm glad you're not a perfect Christian," Preston said.

"Is that right?" She could hear the sarcasm in her voice.

"It's the perfect ones who make me feel I'll never measure up," he said. "My family obviously never did."

"Measure up? No one does that. I'm a prime example of the way God can use damaged, fallible human beings to spread His grace."

He continued to stare into the water. Something else seemed to be bothering him today. In fact, now that she thought about it, aside from the fact that they were all overly stressed about Rick Fenrow, Preston hadn't been himself on this trip.

"Preston?"

"Yeah?"

"You okay?"

He sighed. "I'm fine. I just don't want to fall on my knees and say the sinner's prayer, you know what I mean? I don't know where I'd go if I were to die today, and I don't want to discuss it." He seemed to almost be talking to himself now. "Aren't those the questions a good Christian is supposed to ask someone in order to 'close the deal'?"

"Maybe, but I thought we'd just decided I'm not a good Christian."

He looked at her and grimaced. "Sorry, Ginger." He put an arm over her shoulders and sighed again. "I shouldn't be dragging you into an argument I've been having with someone else."

"Who on earth would have started an argument with you on your sister's wedding day?"

He didn't reply.

And then she thought about the only person whom he might have talked with before breakfast this morning. "Sheila?"

Again, he didn't reply, which was reply enough.

"Okay, I won't pry," Ginger said.

"Good."

"Even though I've taken the brunt of your ire, and earned a good explanation, I have no business involving myself in your relationship with your girlfriend."

"Thank you."

"And even though I've lived longer than you, and have a better understanding of the female psyche, far be it from me to interfere."

"That's fine."

"Even if I might be of help in this situation, I'm sure I don't want to force my advice on you."

He smiled then, and patted her arm before releasing her. "We've got a few days here. Give me some time."

They were silent then, while Graham and Ray were chortling with laughter over something at the front of the boat. Ginger looked at Ray to find him watching her. She didn't look away this time, and neither did he.

Somehow, much of her bitterness had eased, and once again she felt ashamed of her behavior. Here she was trying to convince Preston how sage her advice would be for his relationship with Sheila, and she was behaving like a spoiled child with Ray—had done so for far too long.

She'd known Ray for how many years? Ten? And in all that time, had she ever seen him make any judgments out of spite? No. She had known him to be a man of integrity in every situation. She had thought she'd known his heart. A man like that didn't change overnight.

So why, when one of his difficult decisions involved her, couldn't she trust him? He was the director. He was the one who saw the big picture.

Yes, it hurt badly to know that he felt her incapable of continuing in her former position, but to nurse that hurt, and allow it to hurt others? That was so wrong. She knew better.

Again, she realized that her feelings about him had damaged her professionalism.

She'd been somewhat attracted to him for a long time.

She glanced at him again, then away quickly. Yes, well, so there was a *lot* of attraction. It had been her downfall, obviously.

Though she had never wanted that attraction to cloud her judgment, or to weaken her resolve to be loyal to her mission, obviously it influenced her in an area where she hadn't expected it.

She needed to pray about this more. Best not to go too far with these thoughts yet.

The boat slowed, and Ginger realized they had reached the Fern Grotto, a place renowned for romantic and beautiful weddings.

She looked up into the cave, hung with lush green ferns that formed a natural chapel, and she caught her breath. She turned and looked across the river, at the blue sky crowned with incoming thunderheads to the east.

Yes. Of course. No wonder Willow had chosen this place.

It was worth the trouble.

SEVENTEEN

Ray climbed the stone steps beside Ginger, his hand on her arm in case she should stumble on the uneven surface. Not that she ever would. Except when being knocked sideways by an errant wave, she was as sure-footed as a mountain goat.

He grinned to himself. Ah, yes, Ray Clyde, ever the man who had a way with words. No wonder his friendship with Ginger hadn't developed further in all the years they'd known one another. He wasn't exactly a sweet talker.

Not that he'd have tried to talk her out of a calling from God.

Willow and Graham walked ahead of them with the girls, each holding a child's hand. Something about this moment satisfied something inside Ray—and it wasn't only because he and Ginger were momentarily at peace.

Ginger must have felt it, as well, because she allowed him to hold her arm and guide her.

Halfway up the stairway, she paused and looked up at him. He didn't ask if everything was okay. He could tell from her expression that she, too, felt the rightness of this moment, for Graham and Willow, for the children.

Her eyes filmed with tears, and then she placed her hand over his and continued up the steps.

He contained his surprise. What had suddenly come over her?

Helen and Steve had hired a minister from a local congregation to perform the ceremony. The elderly, native Hawaiian man led the intimate service as if he had done this kind of thing quite a few times. He didn't falter when Graham and Willow explained to him that they had written much of their own ceremony. He seemed overjoyed when they added something to include the children.

Ray had never been more aware of Ginger's presence beside him, her fragrance, her living energy, as he was at this moment. He heard her sniff, and she delicately dabbed at her eyes with a lacy handkerchief.

Ginger had often referred to herself as a sentimental fool, but he loved that about her. No one would ever accuse Ginger Carpenter of being an automaton. She was a human being with a breakable heart.

He had reminded himself countless times that no matter what he had done last year, her heart would still have been broken.

Lucy followed Graham and Willow to the minister who held his Bible in his hand and smiled. Lucy glanced up at Uncle Preston, who winked at her.

Graham and Willow recited the first few words of their ceremony.

Lucy knew those words. She should. She'd listened

to them practice enough times, sitting quietly in the hallway while they worked together to memorize everything. How she'd loved listening to them as they planned this day. They'd laughed and hugged each other any time one of them stuttered or said a wrong word. No yelling or anger.

Willow held up Graham's ring and smiled at him. They stood staring at each other for a few seconds, and she swallowed.

Lucy caught her breath. Oh, no! Willow had forgotten her line! She'd always had trouble with this part.

So Lucy leaned forward and whispered the words to Willow. "Graham, this ring is only a pale symbol—"

Willow glanced down at her and grinned. Graham chuckled. The minister smiled.

"Thank you, sweetheart," Willow whispered, then continued her line.

Graham didn't forget his, of course.

Neither of them forgot anything else, and soon the minister pronounced them husband and wife. Aunt Ginger cried.

Why did grown-ups cry at times like this? There was nothing to cry about, they had so much to celebrate!

When the preacher finally told Graham and Willow they could kiss, Graham picked Willow up and swung her around, and everyone laughed, even Larry Bager.

Lucy felt so good. Of course, she'd seen Graham and Willow kiss before, but this was their first time as married people.

In one more week, they'd all be a family!

Graham and Willow turned to Lucy and Brittany,

knelt on the ground and hugged them. Then Graham pulled a little white box from his pocket and opened it. Inside were two gold chains. Graham took one out and placed it around Brittany's wrist, while Willow did the same with Lucy.

"These are charm bracelets," Graham said. "We thought about getting you rings, but we were afraid you'd outgrow them too quickly. A charm bracelet can have links added to it as you grow, and as more charms are added. We want these bracelets to signify the beginning of our lives together as a family."

Lucy held up her arm and touched the beautiful crystal heart attached to the chain. For the first time she understood why grown-ups cried when they were happy. Because the happiness built up inside until it felt like it might burst. She'd never been happier.

"The beginning of our lives together," Willow murmured softly, then kissed Lucy's cheek.

Ginger dabbed at her tears, wishing the wedding party had more time to linger in the Fern Grotto. This place held her spellbound, the cool, dripping cave with lush, green, lacy ferns hanging from the ceiling of stone. What a beautiful metaphor. By God's grace, life could find its way through the hardest of surfaces when there was opportunity.

She lingered behind the others, watching the girls walk back down the stone steps beside Graham and Willow Vaughn. Though today felt bittersweet to Ginger, she knew the loss of her mothering role with the girls would be worth it in the end. She'd raised her sons successfully into adulthood; it was Willow's turn to enjoy motherhood now.

As Preston and Graham escorted Lucy and Brittany into the boat, Ginger spotted Larry Bager drawing Helen and Steve Courtney aside at the bottom of the stairway.

"It was beautiful, wasn't it?" came a voice behind Ginger that seemed to resonate through the grotto.

She turned and looked up at Ray and nodded, unsure of her own ability to speak at this moment.

"I know this must be difficult for you," he said. "Lucy and Brittany are precious little girls, and you've spent so much time with them."

"So has Willow. We worked things out at the free clinic and at Hideaway Hospital so that Graham, Willow or I could be with them at all times. They needed that special attention this past year."

Another boat half-filled with tourists disgorged its passengers at the dock.

"Would you be interested in a beach walk later tonight?" Ray asked. "I think it's time we had that talk."

"But we've got the luau, and it'll last until long after dark, and—"

"There isn't going to be a luau for us tonight."

She grimaced. "Please don't tell me there's been another glitch."

"Not this time." Ray glanced at the group of newcomers who had started up the steps. He took Ginger's arm as they began their descent. "Our hired bodyguard, Larry, has made the executive decision not only to skip the luau, but to change lodging."

She stopped. "We're leaving the island?"

"Please keep your voice down. We have no idea who might be listening. No, we're not leaving, but we won't return to the hotel."

"Then where will we go?"

Ray leaned closer. "He's arranged for us to stay at the north shore of the island," he said, lowering his voice further.

"Do Steve and Helen know about this?"

"I have a feeling they just found out," he said, nodding toward the couple as they climbed into the boat. "It seems Rick Fenrow has discovered our location."

She felt a tremor of fear. "Oh, Ray, this is all my fault. Why did I leave that calendar up on the wall with all our travel information on it? I should have known better."

Ray put his arm around her and urged her forward again. "I fail to see how you're to blame for the actions of a madman."

"I could have prevented—"

"Stop that. You aren't the culprit here."

"But I knew Fenrow was out of jail, and Lucy was convinced she saw him outside her bedroom window. I kept trying to tell her it was one of her nightmares, and I persuaded myself everything would be okay."

Ray's arm tightened around her shoulders. "Would you stop beating yourself up and listen to me for a minute? Larry hopes to convince Fenrow we've left the island."

The warmth of his arm, his closeness, distracted her. "How…uh…how's Larry going to do that?"

"He's left a trail of misinformation."

"Don't you think we *should* leave?" Ginger asked.

"I know I may sound like a coward, but do you know how wicked this man is?"

"Yes, but I also know that it's easier to keep a lookout for someone in a smaller area. He doesn't know Kauai, and we'll be out of sight. Law enforcement all over the island will be watching for him."

Ginger stopped at the foot of the steps and frowned up at Ray. "Why do I suddenly feel like cheese in a mousetrap?"

"I don't think that's what this is, but wouldn't you rather give him a chance to expose his location here than let him follow all of us back home?"

"We wouldn't necessarily have to go back home," she said. "We could go to California or Montana, New York City or Florida. Lots of places to get lost on the mainland."

"Larry seems to think it would be easier for the police to close in on him here on this island."

She raised her hands in surrender and headed for the boat. "You know what? I disagree, but I'm finished arguing for the day, with anyone."

She'd made enough mistakes in the past two days. Let someone else make the decisions now.

EIGHTEEN

Lucy stared out the back window of the van at the jungle of trees and bushes around them and leaned closer to Aunt Ginger. Brittany sat in front of them beside Uncle Preston, chattering to Chuckles about rivers, mountains and beaches. Larry sat in the front passenger seat, and Helen drove.

Lucy peered over the back of her seat and saw three cars behind them. None were the vehicle she was looking for. "Where are Willow and Graham and Ray?"

Helen glanced at her in the rear-view mirror. "They'll be along shortly. Steve wanted to stop and get some steaks and salad fixings in Princeville. Now that we have a kitchen, but no restaurant nearby, I plan to cook some of my famous gourmet meals."

Every few seconds, Lucy caught a flicker of ocean waves and a streak of sand to the right of the road, past the trees. "We can't swim in that water," she told Aunt Ginger softly. "The waves are too high."

"Let's hope they won't be so high all the time we're here," Aunt Ginger said. "After the storm, things should calm down, and I've heard there's a good place to snorkel near here."

"Did you all know we're staying at the edge of a rain forest?" Helen glanced at Lucy again in the mirror. "There's a mountain near here that gets more daily rain than any other place on the planet."

Lucy grimaced. Rain? Storms? Rough water? Why would anyone want to spend their vacation in this place? "Why did we have to come here?" she muttered to Aunt Ginger under her breath. "We can't swim, can't snorkel."

Helen glanced in the mirror again. "That mountain rain is farther inland, a couple of mountains away."

Lucy frowned at her. Why was Helen listening to everything she said?

"Don't worry, sweetie," Helen continued. "Maybe you'll get to do some snorkeling at Anini Beach before we have to fly back home. That's only a short drive away. We might all want to take a hiking expedition while we're here."

"There's a hiking trail?" Aunt Ginger asked.

"Sure is," Helen said. "We're close to the Kalalau Trail on the Napali Coastline, though that trail isn't recommended for children. It's slick, and there are dangerous drops from the cliffs. Lots of wilderness in these mountains, though, so we could find another trail. Oopsie, here's the address." She turned into a muddy, narrow driveway half-overgrown with tall bushes that brushed the windows of the van, like green arms reaching out.

Lucy stared into the shadows of those bushes. This place looked scary. And wet. "I guess nobody's going to find us here, are they?"

Aunt Ginger put an arm around her and drew her close. "It looks like a pretty good hiding place, if you ask me."

"But what if they find us anyway?" Lucy whispered. "There's nobody around to save us."

Aunt Ginger sighed, but she didn't say anything. That worried Lucy.

"Larry, didn't you speak to the owner about opening the house?" Helen asked.

"Yes, and the hotel staff who brought our things were supposed to open the windows and air it out. There are six bedrooms and four bathrooms, two living areas, a game room and a deck on the roof."

"Is there a swimming pool?" Lucy asked.

"With a beach barely two hundred feet away?" Larry asked. "Not hardly."

"It should be wonderful!" Helen's voice sounded too cheerful. "As soon as we get settled, I can send Steve back to the store to stock up while I start dinner."

Lucy turned in her seat to see if Steve was following with Graham and Willow and Ray, but the overgrown bushes had closed in behind them, swallowing them.

The van plunged from the trees into a wide clearing beside a huge gray house that stood high above the ground on thick columns, set back against a tall mountain.

"It's got stilts!" Brittany exclaimed.

"That's to protect from storm surges," Helen said as she pulled beneath the house and parked.

"What's a storm surge?" Brittany asked.

"Back home in Missouri, we call them floods," Helen replied.

"But here they're like huge waves that blast everything in their path," Lucy said. "Like when there's a hurricane or tropical storm, and the ocean drowns—"

Aunt Ginger pressed her fingers over Lucy's lips and gave her a warning look.

"Sweethearts," Helen said, "this house is so high off the ground, I doubt any storm surge could reach it. And it looks like we'll have a great view of the ocean from the deck on the roof. Larry, how did you come up with this place on such short notice?"

"I asked around," he said. "This time of year a lot of vacation places are empty."

"I want to go see the waves!" Brittany cried as she scrambled for the door and tried to open it.

"Hold it for a minute, okay?" Larry got out and slid the door back for her. "Give us some time to settle."

Brittany took Larry's hand, still clutching Chuckles. "Can we go see those flowers over there?" She turned back to Uncle Preston. "Come on, Uncle Preston, I see a pond. Let's go see if there's fish!"

"Why don't I take the girls for a little walk," Helen suggested to Aunt Ginger. "We can go down and check out the shoreline, maybe look for some shells while Steve helps the rest of you—"

Lucy gasped. "No!" She turned to Aunt Ginger. "Don't let her do it, Aunt Ginger. Please don't let her take us!"

Ginger stared with surprise into Lucy's frightened face, then cast a confused look at Helen, who met her gaze in the rear-view mirror. The woman's shoulders slumped as she closed her eyes and sighed.

What's going on here?

"Sweetheart," Ginger said to Lucy, "why are you so frightened? Helen won't let anything happen to you."

"She might," Lucy muttered under her breath.

"I think you're afraid of Rick Fenrow, aren't you? Do you think Helen won't be able to protect you from him? If that's the problem, Larry can go with you, too."

"No, Ginger," Helen said as she opened the driver door and slid out from behind the steering wheel. "I don't think that's the problem." She closed the door and circled the van.

Lucy stiffened and clutched Ginger's arm. "I don't want to go with her," she whispered. "I'm scared of her."

"Why?"

"She and Steve knew my mother, and they're keeping it a secret."

"What do you mean? How could they have known your mother?"

"I heard them talking." Lucy glanced at Helen, who stood outside the van with her arms crossed, watching Larry and Preston with Brittany. "She and Steve were talking about Mama, and she said her name, like she knew her." Lucy looked up at Ginger. "She shouldn't know my mother. Why would wedding people know my mother? Why didn't they say anything? Don't let them be alone with us, Aunt Ginger."

"I won't let anyone hurt you, honey. You know that." Something was definitely strange about this, and it wasn't Lucy's overactive imagination. Helen didn't seem surprised by Lucy's behavior, she seemed upset.

But she didn't look dangerous to Ginger.

At last, Steve arrived with the rest of the wedding

party. He pulled the Xterra beneath the house and parked. Laughter spilled from the open driver's window, but Steve sobered when his wife rushed to intercept him as soon as he opened his door.

She spoke a few quiet words to him, and he looked over at Lucy as she climbed from the van.

He nodded and turned to intercept Graham as he and Willow stepped from the vehicle. Ray got out of the passenger seat, and the smile on his face died.

Then Helen turned back to Lucy. "Honey, I think you and I need to have a little talk." When Lucy started to protest, she continued, "It's okay, Graham and Willow will be with us." She sighed, looking tired, even haggard. This trip had not been easy on any of them.

The four adults walked with Lucy toward the outdoor staircase that led to the upstairs entryway. Brittany continued to explore the grounds with Preston and Larry, chattering about the mountain with all the rain.

Ray circled the SUV to Ginger's side, looking thoughtful. "What do you say to a little exploring?"

"What do you want to explore?"

"How about the roof deck? I saw a stairway at the side of the house, and I bet that's where it leads."

"Aren't you even curious about what's going on with Helen and Steve?"

Ray watched the front door close behind Lucy and her adult companions. "I'm sure Willow and Lucy will fill you in on all the details," he teased. "What do you say? Explore?"

"Guess I could." She glanced at Larry and Preston,

who were occupying themselves with an inspection of a flowering shrub with brilliant red flowers.

Brittany now rode on Preston's shoulders, and she had Chuckles perched on Preston's head. That man would be a good father someday.

Ginger turned back to Ray. It was time for some major apologies.

He held his hand out. "Come with me?"

She took it. "I'd love to."

Lucy refused to cling to Willow or Graham as they followed Helen and Steve into the house. Why wasn't Larry with them? Didn't he know they could be in danger? She wanted to call out to him, but when she turned to look back down the stairs, he and Uncle Preston and Brittany were busy checking out some flowers at the edge of the yard. Aunt Ginger and Ray stood by the van, talking.

Steve opened the double doors of the house and pushed them wide for the others to enter.

Helen paused on the threshold and caught her breath. "Would you look at this gorgeous place! Steve, I've always wanted to decorate our living room with bolder colors. And look at this beautiful hardwood floor! Someone invested a little cash in this place."

Lucy didn't really like the wood floors. She liked soft, thick carpets that a kid could lie on while watching TV. But there wasn't a TV in this living room, there was just Helen and Steve.

Helen suggested they all sit at the dining room table, at the far end of the huge living room.

The wooden tabletop was so shiny Lucy could almost see her reflection in it—and Graham's and Willow's as she hurried to the chair between them.

Steve pulled open some blinds along the wall to reveal a huge window that overlooked a garden in back, at the foot of the mountain. A narrow road wound up the side of the mountain. Lucy wondered who ever drove up that road. Or who drove down it from the top. Maybe it was a hiking trail.

"Something unfortunate happened this morning that we need to explain." Helen pulled out a chair across the table from Lucy and sat down. "Honey, you overheard me say something that could have been taken wrong. I never meant to frighten you."

Lucy watched her sit down. Steve patted his wife's shoulder, and a look passed between them. What were they up to?

"You knew my mother," Lucy said.

Helen nodded her head. "Yes, I did."

"What?" Willow exclaimed.

"You knew Sandi?" Graham asked. "And you never told us about it?"

"You told Steve that you would never forgive Sandi for what she did to us girls," Lucy said. "And then he said you didn't have a choice because she was dead now, and then you said it didn't have to be that way."

Willow caught her breath, and reached for Lucy's hand.

Graham placed his arm over the back of Lucy's chair. "I think it's time for some explanations." His words were suddenly clipped and hard. "And you might try telling us why you're on this trip under false pretenses."

"Please," Steve said, "this isn't what it seems."

"So it isn't a cover-up?" Graham asked.

Steve and Helen looked at each other, then Helen said, "We really are exotic wedding planners and travel guides. I've been a professional photographer for thirty-five years."

"I ran our travel agency until five years ago," Steve said, "when we decided on a change."

"Taking this job with you was my idea," Helen said. "The only difference between this job and any other is that we aren't as familiar with this island as we are with the others, and with islands in the Caribbean. That's why we've had the glitches here, and for that, we apologize." Her gaze rested on Lucy. "And we have a special interest in two of our young clients."

Willow squeezed Lucy's hand reassuringly. "Helen, why? Who are you?"

Helen clasped her hands together on the table. "Sandi was my niece."

For a moment there was no sound at the table. Lucy stared at Helen, then looked at Steve as he placed an arm around his wife's shoulders.

"You were right, honey," Helen said to him softly. "We shouldn't've come, but I couldn't resist. It was such an opportunity to spend time with the girls."

"Brittany and I don't have any relatives," Lucy said. "Mama told us."

"Oh, but you do," Steve said. "Your mama had twenty-two first cousins on her mother's side. Your grandmother had three brothers and four sisters. Helen was the oldest sister, and Jennifer, your grandmother, was the youngest."

Lucy stared at him. Why should she believe this stranger? "Why didn't I know my grandmother?"

"Jennifer died of an...she died when Sandi was twenty," Helen said.

"Like mother, like daughter," Steve said.

"What do you mean?" Lucy asked.

"I mean your mother followed in her own mother's footsteps. She was a—"

"I think that's explanation enough," Graham said. "I suppose you have proof of your relationship?"

"I have pictures in my suitcase," Helen said. "We have letters and copies of medical records, all of which can be authenticated."

"Sandi cut us both out of Lucy's and Brittany's lives when they were tiny," Steve explained. "Brittany was in diapers."

"And now look at what's happened to Sandi," Helen said, holding her hands out to Willow and Graham in an expression of helplessness. "I did all I could, but I was too outspoken about her lifestyle, and she didn't appreciate it any more than her mother did."

"Why did you bring authentication with you?" Willow asked. "Why, exactly, did you agree to book our group?"

"Wouldn't you have taken any opportunity to spend time with your little great-nieces if you had the chance?" Helen asked. "Especially if you've never been allowed to do so before?"

"You wanted to be close to the girls, I understand that," Willow said. "But why didn't you identify yourselves to us in the first place?"

"We weren't sure what your reaction would be," Helen said. "We didn't know you then. What would you have said if we'd marched up to your front door and told you who we were, and that we wanted to check you out?"

"We would have thought you were going to try to stop the adoption," Graham said.

Lucy gasped and jumped from her chair. "No! You can't do that!"

Graham caught her gently, and pulled her onto his lap, wrapping his arms firmly around her. "The adoption has been approved, Steve. You can't possibly expect to—"

"We aren't planning to do anything now that we've seen you with them," Helen said. "Don't you worry about that. But you must understand why we were worried. We only found out about Sandi's death in early November. Sandi had changed her last name, and she had done everything she could to make sure no one could track her down."

"We wanted to make sure Lucy and Brittany would have a good home," Steve said, looking at Lucy. "This time."

"Steve and I might be a little old to be raising two little girls," Helen said. "Steve has a heart condition. But we'd planned to do that, if necessary. We failed them when Sandi was alive, but we couldn't fail them now."

NINETEEN

Ray leaned against the deck railing beside Ginger and watched the waves crash against the rocky shore beyond the trees. The woman beside him held more fascination for him than the beauty of the island—which was considerable here on Kauai's northernmost tip.

The late afternoon sunlight turned stray strands of Ginger's short, wavy hair into smoking flames. He was the moth.

"Ginger," he said softly, "you look lost in thought."

She nodded, still watching those waves. "You know how, back in the days of the wild, wild West, pioneers in a wagon train banded together for safety on their trip? And they circled the wagons when threatened?"

Ray thought about Rick Fenrow and understood what she meant. "Even when some of those wagoners might have been adversaries and set sparks off one another during the trek west?"

"Even then," she said.

"But then maybe they discovered that there's safety in numbers, and the enemy wasn't who they perceived it to be in the first place."

"I don't see you as my enemy, Ray."

He smiled. "Since when?"

"I never should have. I know who the real enemy is on this trip. Rick Fenrow destroys lives, not just careers."

Ray winced.

"Okay, I didn't mean…let me rephrase that," she said. "I wasn't—"

"Too late. Ginger, I didn't ever want to—"

"I know." She reached out and took his hand.

It startled him, but he certainly wouldn't protest.

"I had a heart-to-heart with God about *my* response to your presence on this trip," she said. "I behaved like a spoiled child, and I set a blasphemous example for the children to see."

He quirked a brow at her "*Blasphemous?* Where on earth did you come up with that? Unfortunate, maybe, or crude, but I wouldn't call it blasphemous."

She gave him a wry look and tried to pull her hand away.

He held it fast. "You're not a spoiled child, Ginger. You're a woman who has strong opinions, and you're a wonderful example for the children."

For a moment, she studied the waves, then she looked up at him. "In that case, don't you think I'm mature enough to know the truth behind the changes you made last year?"

"You're mature enough." With slow, deliberate movements, he raised her hand and traced the outlines of her fingers. "I think maybe the problem has been my own lack of maturity."

"You can't be serious," she said in a flat tone.

He looked down into those beautiful, guileless

eyes, and felt such an ache of remorse. He had treated her like a child last year. Who could wonder at her anger?

Yet, there was hope. Last year the truth might have injured her far worse than it would now, with some time for memories to fade, and attachments to loosen their hold.

"What is it, Ray?"

He swallowed, then drew her to two deck chairs that had a perfect view of the blue horizon over the treetops. "Have a seat."

She did as she was asked for, perhaps, the first time on this trip, and he was forced, at last, to release her hand.

She settled beside him. As if bracing for what might be coming, she leaned back in the chair and gazed into the distance. "I should have realized from the beginning that you had a good reason for what you did." She looked up at him, then back at the ocean. "I knew your heart, Ray. But I felt so...rejected."

"Believe me, nothing could be further from the truth."

"So why don't you tell me the truth?"

He sighed. He could do this. It was time. He would tell her the whole truth.

Ginger felt as if she was nearing the end of a free fall, and she was about to splatter on the ground. But she'd asked for this moment for too long. What could be worse than what she'd already believed to be true?

A muscle worked in Ray's jaw, a sure sign of tension.

He cleared his throat. "I received an anonymous call last February from someone warning me that your life might be in danger."

She caught her breath, unable to conceal her shock. "My *life?* In Belarus?"

He nodded.

She swallowed. "That kind of thing happened from time to time. *That's* why you brought me back to Missouri? Ray, missionaries face danger like that every day. There were other lives besides mine at stake. And there were souls at stake. You didn't think I could handle that news?"

He shook his head. "I wasn't even sure I could handle it. I was frantic. I considered shutting down the clinic completely, or turning it over to the Belarusians and pulling out the entire American staff."

She straightened in her chair. "Of course you couldn't do that! Think how many people were dependent on that clinic. They need—"

"I found out who made the call." His voice suddenly softened.

She studied his expression. "Okay."

"Nicolai."

She caught her breath, feeling a stab of anguish. One of her children? "Which one? Nick or Colya?" She had given those two boys nicknames when they first came to the clinic because they were both named Nicolai.

"He had blond hair and blue eyes and was skinny as a fence post," Ray said.

"That would be Colya." She felt another squeeze of anguish. She couldn't suppress the tears that sprang to her eyes. Charming, friendly Colya, who had always been so eager to please, so affectionate. "He threatened my...my life?"

"He warned me that your life might be in danger. Big difference."

The anguish eased. Not her Colya, then. *Thank you, Jesus.* Colya was one of the kids who had spent so much time hanging around the clinic, helping out with odd jobs and translations. Even as a ten-year-old, he knew enough English to translate for her when she was still learning Russian.

"But why didn't he tell me?" she asked. "I could have dealt with it."

"No, you couldn't." Ray's voice sharpened. "He knew if he told you about it, you'd come right out and confront the culprit, and he was afraid for his own life, as well as yours."

"He told you that?"

"In person, when I flew to Minsk."

"With my replacement?"

"No, I flew out myself before I would risk the life of any replacement."

"When did you do that?"

"As soon as you arrived home. I used your heart arrhythmia as an excuse to get you back home so I could investigate the threat," he said. "I wanted to handle it as quietly as possible."

She felt another emotion coming into play. Utter humiliation. Because she had a reputation for not keeping her mouth shut, Ray had been forced to go behind her back? And Colya had done so, as well?

"I know I'm not the most cautious person on the mission field," she said. "And I've never been subtle with my opinions, but—"

"You are who you are, Ginger, and no one would want you any other way. However, I couldn't take that chance, either as your director, or as someone who cares very much for you."

She clasped her hands together and stared down at them. "Who threatened me?"

He took a deep breath, let it out. "Sergei."

She sprang to her feet, returned to the deck railing and gripped it tightly. "No."

"You know how close Colya was to him. I had a bad feeling about it as soon as I got the call."

"Isn't it possible Colya might have been exaggerating a little? Sergei had a bad temper, and said things in the heat of anger that he didn't really—"

"Don't excuse his behavior. What happened between you and Sergei last winter that made him so angry? And why didn't you tell me about it? Colya didn't know, and Sergei wouldn't tell him."

Oh, yes. Last winter. Maybe she hadn't handled that as well as she'd thought. "I caught him early one morning in the clinic, trying to break into the drug cabinet. I gave him a firm talking-to, and he responded with childish bravado. I banned him from the clinic for two weeks, and thought that was the end of it. When he came back he apologized. I hugged him and invited him to dinner and thought things were fine."

"Not the most insightful thing you've ever done," Ray said. "Colya told me Sergei had been talking wildly one night after he'd drank a half bottle of vodka, and he betrayed thoughts about murdering you."

Ginger felt a renewed stab of pain, sharp and wicked.

"I can't believe Sergei would ever have followed through with any of his threats."

"Exactly. That's why I brought you home, because you wouldn't have believed it, and would have made things worse if I'd told you."

She heard him get up, and he joined her at the railing.

"I also knew that if you had realized what was going on last year, you'd have been devastated," he said.

"But I was." She looked up at him.

"I realize that."

"Those boys were the ones I felt I had betrayed when I didn't get to return to Belarus."

"I believed it would be better for you to be angry with me for a while than to be hurt by Sergei's deception and hatred."

She felt tears sting her eyes. After all this time, all this blame she'd placed on Ray, and she had been wrong.

And how could Sergei have felt that way about her? She'd loved those boys, taken them into her home, time after time, when their own parents were busy working. She had fed them, given them motherly advice. Yes, she'd been firm with them, but no more so than she'd been with her own children.

"Sergei has since been in trouble with the police, Ginger," Ray said. "He's in prison now."

She felt her face crumple. "Oh, Ray."

He took her into his arms and held her while she soaked the front of his shirt with tears and a good portion of her makeup.

"That poor, struggling child! I've known him since he was eight."

"I know," he soothed.

"He lived with his mother and a bully of an older brother."

"That's what Colya told me," Ray said.

"When things got too hard to deal with at home—which they often did—he came to the clinic, or to my apartment over the clinic."

"You did everything you could for him," Ray assured her, his deep voice wrapping its comfort—its forgiveness—around her.

All remaining bitterness drained from her, and she allowed herself to grieve her loss, this time without anger. Where had she gone wrong with Sergei? And how could she have handled the situation so that the whole mission clinic wouldn't have been in danger of being shut down, or the Americans sent home?

"All these years," she said, "I thought that if I loved enough, gave enough of myself, forgave enough and tried hard enough, things would always work out."

"How do you know they haven't?"

She frowned. "They obviously haven't for Sergei."

"I don't think God's finished with him yet," Ray said.

"I thought I was running a successful program over there, and that God was blessing it."

"He is, and you set the foundation for that. Look at all who've been helped."

"I didn't take the opposition into account," she said. "God can bless, but people can make bad choices."

"God's blessings have a way of diversifying with the choices people make, Ginger. Actually, it's been my experience that sometimes, under the most opposition,

God's blessings multiply exponentially. You may see your return home from Belarus as a failure, but I see it as an opportunity for you to lay a future foundation."

"That's all well and good, but what about Sergei? Things certainly didn't turn out for him."

"You sowed a lot of seeds with him. Now it's time to let others do the gardening and reaping."

She sighed. Now he was trying to make her feel better. "I'm so sorry, Ray. After all our years of friendship, how could I have doubted your heart? I knew you better than that."

"And I should have been honest with you from the beginning," he said. "Maybe that speaks of my own inability to trust."

"But you were probably right not to."

He leaned back and gazed at her. His own dark blue eyes filled with sudden amusement. He broke into a smile and drew back. "We could each recite a long list of regrets, couldn't we?"

"I know I could."

"But the past is just that. It's over. Let's learn from it and go on."

"Okay," she said. "Where do we go from here?"

He cocked his head to the side and smiled slightly. "You really want to know what I think?"

She nodded.

The smile widened. "I'm glad you asked. There's something I've wanted to do for years." He cupped her cheek with his hand, and before she realized what he had in mind, he lowered his head and pressed his lips gently to hers.

Startled, she caught her breath and jerked back. "Ray?"

"Hey, lovebirds!" called Larry from the top of the steps. "Hate to interrupt things, but I've got some good news."

Ginger stepped away from Ray, heart pounding, stunned by his kiss, and her immediate, shocked response.

"Got word from the police in Lihue," Larry said. "They have a suspect in custody who matches Fenrow's description."

"They have Fenrow?" Ray exclaimed.

Larry nodded. "They got a tip from someone at the hotel that he was hanging around the fourth floor hallway, and didn't have any reason to be there." He punched his fist into the air. "I think we've got our man! I'm on my way there to make sure."

Ray laughed. "Want me to come with you?"

Larry turned to retreat down the stairs. "Not on your life. Go ahead and return to what you were doing. Don't let me stand in the way of romance. Graham and Willow are coming with me, and as soon as we ID Fenrow, they're going to rent another car and take off for a few days as originally planned."

"What about the storm tonight?" Ray called after him.

"I don't think they'll get out in it, do you? I'll be back before it hits." He chuckled all the way down the stairs.

Ginger grabbed Ray in a bear hug, and this time, when he kissed her, she returned his passion with all the enthusiasm with which she had hurled her anger. Their trip wouldn't be ruined, after all.

TWENTY

Lucy walked beside Aunt Ginger across the road and between the trees as Uncle Preston and Brittany raced to see who would reach the beach first. Of course, Uncle Preston would let Brittany win. He always did, which Lucy didn't think was a good idea. Brittany would think she was really a good runner when she wasn't.

Lucy could beat her, she just chose not to.

"Don't get too far out into the water, you two," Aunt Ginger called after them. "Remember how rough it is."

Uncle Preston waved at her without looking back. Lucy knew Brittany was safe with him.

Aunt Ginger rested a hand on Lucy's shoulder. "Helen told me what the meeting was about. I guess you were pretty shocked."

Lucy nodded.

"How do you feel about having relatives you didn't know you had?"

Lucy tensed as she watched Brittany plunge into the shallows without stopping to see what was under the water. There could be sharp rocks or shells, eels or stingrays.

"Don't want to talk about it?" Aunt Ginger asked.

Lucy shrugged. "I don't trust them."

"You don't think they're telling the truth?"

Lucy looked up at Aunt Ginger then, and reached for her hand. When she had it, she squeezed tightly with both of her own. "Maybe they are, but what if they try to stop the adoption? They said they wouldn't, but what if they do? And what if they try to force us to go live with them instead of Graham and Willow, and they're really mean? What if we never get to see you and Graham and Willow and Uncle Preston again, and they take us far, far away and beat us and—"

"Whoa, there, my dear." Aunt Ginger stopped and dropped to her knees. She reached up and framed both sides of Lucy's face with her hands. "Would you please slow down? You should probably be a novelist when you grow up, because you have a vivid imagination."

Lucy wanted to cry. But she didn't. She wanted to wrap her arms around Aunt Ginger's neck and hold on tight and never let her go. "I'm...s-scared."

Aunt Ginger gently placed her fingers on Lucy's chin and held her gaze. "We've all been scared for a couple of days because of the news about Rick Fenrow's escape. Now, suddenly that threat is gone, but I don't think we realize it yet. Do you think maybe you're trying to replace one fear with another?"

Lucy frowned at her. "Huh?"

"Fear can be habit forming, and the fear we've felt since we heard about that man's prison escape has been difficult for us to deal with. Don't let that fear continue now that the scare is over."

"I've been afraid for a long time," Lucy said. "Sometimes I was afraid when Mama left us alone at night, and sometimes I was afraid when she didn't."

"Oh, honey." Aunt Ginger drew Lucy into her arms and snuggled her close. "I know. It's going to be different from now on, and you'll soon learn that."

"That's why I need you to tell me the truth when I'm scared, not tell me I don't have anything to worry about."

Aunt Ginger sighed. "Okay, I'll admit I noticed that Helen has watched you a lot on this trip, and I wondered about it a couple of times, but sometimes we women get all gooshy when we're around children. I had the impression that she wished she had little girls like you and Brittany so she could shower you with love. Mean people don't get all misty-eyed around little kids, they get cranky. I never once saw Helen cranky."

Lucy shrugged. "Maybe not." But Aunt Ginger had been wrong when she said Rick Fenrow hadn't been standing in the window of Lucy's bedroom back home. What if she was wrong about this?

Finally, after a long, woman-to-woman talk with Lucy about the relative safety of this beach, Ginger convinced the worrywart to join Brittany in the sand of the sheltered cove. Then she and Preston attacked a few waves with inept attempts to body surf—he'd been right, the water was too rough—before retreating to a rocky rise so they could have a better view of the beach as they watched the girls play.

The cloud bank, which had been slowly advancing all afternoon from the east, had nearly covered the sky, though the sun shone with warmth near the western horizon.

There was a protected swimming area only a few hundred feet south along the shoreline. Maybe another day, when the water was more peaceful, Ginger would take the girls snorkeling. She only hoped that would happen before they had to go back home.

Ginger had noticed a campground on the drive to the house earlier, and she'd seen some swimmers floating facedown on the choppy waters, snorkels in the air. Helen had spoken about the bounty of tropical fish along these shores.

Ginger perched atop a jut of rock so she would have no trouble seeing the girls from where she sat. "Ever been a lifeguard?"

Preston shook his head. He had sunk once more into his morose mood after the wedding ceremony. He covered it well when he was with the girls.

He slumped down beside her.

"You've been on the phone with Sheila again," Ginger guessed.

"I'm not sure you can call it a phone conversation, since we lost the connection three times, and she finally gave up and told me we'd talk about it when I got home."

"Ever thought of trying to use a landline and charging it to your credit card?" Ginger asked. "It's an option. I know it's probably more expensive, but if she's worth it to you—"

"The question isn't whether or not she's worth it to me, I think she's telling me I'm not worth it to her."

"Why don't you stop telling me how you feel, and tell me what she actually said," Ginger suggested.

Preston was not known for his comprehension skills, especially when it came to women.

He spread his hands. "What's to tell? She's a bona fide, Bible believing Christian, and I'm not. End of story. Nice girls like her don't date bad boys like me, who don't pay homage to her God."

"*That's* what she actually said?" Ginger asked.

"No, she implied that we were at cross-purposes, and would stay that way until I had a change of heart."

Ginger felt badly for Preston. He'd been smitten long before his release from the hospital last year. Sheila was an excellent nurse, who gave tender care to all her patients, but her tender care had turned into more between her and Preston.

"You know, I don't like to say I told you so," Ginger said, "but one reason I've always been concerned about doctor-patient personal relationships is because patients tend to experience a heightened sense of need that can lead to a strong, unhealthy attachment to their caregiver."

She thought about what she'd said for a moment and wondered if that same psychology might have been the case with Colya, Nick and Sergei. Had she encouraged them to form an unhealthy attachment to her because she had cared for their health needs for so long?

Could she have identified and worked on Sergei's personal limitations sooner if she hadn't been so emotionally involved?

"Those relationships don't always last once the patient has healed, because they don't reflect reality," she continued.

"Well, excuse me, Miss Manners, but that isn't the

situation with Sheila," Preston said. "It looks as if God's out to get me because I'm not preaching on the street corners for him."

"He's not out to get you."

Preston rolled his eyes at her. "You're not the best at this, are you? Every person who ever tried to get me 'saved' has tried to convince me that God *is* out to get me."

She grimaced. "Okay, fine, He *is* out to get you, but only because He loves you and wants you to be happy with Him in your life."

"Preaching again," Preston chided.

"I'm a missionary, I preach. Look, Preston, maybe you don't need to force the issue with Sheila right now. I think this situation needs a gentle touch."

"Gentle touch?"

"That's right." Ginger glanced down toward the girls. Brittany had not ventured back into the water. Lucy hadn't even taken off her shoes. "Have you ever brought home a bag of salad or potato chips that you found hard to open? You jerk on the package and fumble with the bag until you overpower it, and at the moment of triumph, chips or salad fixings go flying all over the kitchen counter."

Preston raised his eyebrows. "Are you trying to go somewhere with this? Because you haven't arrived yet."

"Don't interrupt. Someone could take that same bag, pull it open gently, and have no trouble with flying food."

"And that would be why?"

She shrugged. "I don't know much about applied force. All I'm saying is I've found that a gentle, non-threatening touch can get a point across a lot more easily than force. The cellophane bag is a fine example of human interaction. No one wants to be browbeaten into submission. You know that by your own experiences when someone tries to force you to come to Christ. People need to be led gently."

"I don't need anything, and I don't see what cellophane packaging has to do with Sheila and me."

"Okay, look, all Sheila is trying to tell you is that God works out relationships. He is the strength that keeps marriages together. Love Him first, and allow everything else to follow."

"Aha! There it is," Preston said. "You're saying I must love God before I can love Sheila."

"Think that sounds harsh?" she asked. "When He is the one Who can make any relationship work, can make it rich with love and friendship and goodness? Is that so bad?"

"It is when He's held over my head like a bludgeon."

"That isn't what Sheila is doing. She knows that God can make so much more out of a romance than two people can make of it without Him."

"So you're saying I might want to use a more gentle approach with Sheila."

"Excuse me? Isn't that what I just said? Were you even listening?"

He looked intrigued. "Mind if I take a stab at it now? I'll go back to the house, use the landline and talk to Sheila as if she were a cellophane bag of salad. No, make that potato chips."

"You're such a romantic."

A child's scream jolted them both to their feet.

Ginger caught sight of a renegade wave seconds before it splashed her in the face, all the way up on the rock.

"Grab the girls!" Preston shouted as he leaped from the rocks into the churning water.

TWENTY-ONE

Lucy dug her heels into the sand and jerked hard on Brittany's arm, choking as the salty water spurted up her nose. Her eyes stung, and she couldn't see or hear anything, just felt the water trying to force her and Brittany out to sea.

Another wave knocked her down. She tumbled backward and lost her grip on Brittany's arm. She couldn't get her head out of the water and she didn't know which way was up. Above the rumble of water, she heard her sister scream, and then she felt hands grabbing her.

She gasped for breath, choking and gagging on sand in her mouth. Someone held her in his or her arms, hugging her, brushing hair from her face.

"It's okay, honey, I've got you."

Aunt Ginger. Lucy opened eyes that stung with salt-water. "Brittany! I lost her!"

Then she saw Uncle Preston, carrying Brittany out of the surf. She was screaming, holding her right elbow.

"Let's get off this beach!" Uncle Preston called. "This water's wild."

Brittany kept screaming as they ran toward the house.

Lucy wriggled to get down. "What's wrong with her? What happened?"

Aunt Ginger set her on her feet in the sand and rushed to check on Brittany, who screamed louder when Aunt Ginger touched her right arm.

"Shhh, hush, honey, it's okay. I'm not going to hurt you," Aunt Ginger soothed. "What happened? What hurts? Did you hit your elbow on something?"

Brittany shook her head. "The water jerked me and Lucy held on, but it kept grabbing me and wouldn't let go, and…" Her face scrunched. "It hurt me."

"Let me check it." Aunt Ginger took Brittany's hand as if she was going to shake hands with her, then touched the inside of her arm.

Brittany howled, and Lucy rushed to her. "You're going to be okay. Aunt Ginger'll take care of you." Like she always did to calm Brittany, Lucy rubbed her sister's forehead, then smoothed back her hair, while Aunt Ginger grasped Brittany's wrist and bent her arm.

Brittany screamed again, and Lucy winced.

"I'm done, sweetheart," Aunt Ginger said. "Your arm's fixed. It'll stop hurting in a few seconds."

Brittany cried for a moment, and then she looked down at her elbow and straightened her arm. Her eyes widened.

Lucy looked up at Aunt Ginger. "What happened?"

"She got what we call nursemaid's elbow. I wasn't sure, because she's a little old for it, but when someone accidentally jerks a little child's arm too hard, it can pull a bone out of position. I put it back in place."

Lucy examined the elbow again. It looked fine. "I was the one who hurt her?" Willow and Aunt Ginger were always telling her not to hold on to Brittany so much, not to pull on her and grab her. "I did that?"

Aunt Ginger looked down at her and smiled. "Now, you tell me, young lady, what do you think Brittany would have preferred, nursemaid's elbow or being washed out to sea? You're our little heroine, my dear. You might have saved Brittany's life!"

Ray knelt in front of the dining room chair where Brittany sat, and gently checked the movement of her right elbow. "It looks perfect," he told Ginger. "Of course, I'm not surprised." He looked up at Helen, who had come running as soon as she saw Preston and Ginger carrying the girls to the house. "I don't suppose we have anything around here that could function as a sling, do we?"

Helen brightened and snapped her fingers. "I know just the thing. Lucy, what do you think the hotel staff did this afternoon with that wrap I gave you to wear over your swimsuit?

"I saw it in my top drawer in our bedroom."

"I think we could make a sling out of that, don't you? And I'll buy you an even prettier wrap."

As Lucy and Helen went to get the sling, Ginger pulled Brittany onto her lap.

Ray couldn't keep his eyes off Ginger. "You still have the touch," he said.

She grinned at him. "It isn't as if I went to seed this past year. I've been busy. I still know my job."

Brittany tapped Ginger's arm. "Aunt Ginger, can we go hiking now? You said we could, and Lucy wants to hike that road behind this house. Can we go?"

Ginger laughed. "Honey, you just got attacked by a monster wave, you've been injured, and your arm will be in a sling. Why don't we take it easy and watch a movie tonight?"

"I want to go hiking. Please? Lucy wants to see what's up the mountain, and you said she saved my life. She should get to do what she wants tonight."

Ginger looked at Ray. "What do you think, Doctor Clyde? Should our patient be allowed to hike in the Kauai rain forest after her injury?"

"I don't see why not, if you can pack three umbrellas in case the rain gets here before you can make it back. They've been drenched in the ocean already, so I don't see how a little more water could hurt them."

"At least Brittany can't be attacked by another wave up on the mountainside," Ginger said. "It should be perfectly safe."

Ginger felt Brittany's hair, then her clothes. "We need to change first. We all got a good soaking. Then we need to find our backpacks. You shouldn't carry one, Brittany, but Lucy and I will, and we'll need flashlights, in case anything happens and we don't get back before dark."

"Try to make sure that doesn't happen," Ray said.

Brittany scrambled down from her chair and ran through the house, calling for Lucy.

Ray looked at Ginger. Helen had fired up the grill outside, and smoke drifted past the window. Steve had gone back to the store for groceries for the week. It promised to be a laid-back, comfortable stay, safe from their stalker, and far enough from the water that they would have no worries in the storm.

"You realize, don't you, that when I say hike, I'm thinking of a short thirty-minute stroll up the hill and back," he said.

"Or less."

"Because in spite of all the reassurances I keep getting about this storm coming in, I can't help remembering the last tropical storm here wiped out most of the signs to Poipu."

"The last weather report I heard had downgraded the storm even further, Ray, and it isn't supposed to hit us for at least a couple of hours. We'll be back before you know it." She leaned forward and put a hand over his. "Lucy is such a little trouper, and she's been tense this whole trip. If she wants to go on a hike, I want to take her. You could come with us, you know."

He looked down at their hands, then glanced outside at the track that she and the girls would be following up the mountain. Sometimes the responsibilities of his job weighed heavily. "May I take a rain check on that? We've had a situation at our clinic in Kobrin that I have to address immediately."

"Oh? Kobrin?" Her hand tightened on his. "Are Jacque and Marti okay?"

"They're fine, but Marti called a few minutes ago about a suspected flu epidemic, and he's low on supplies. Minsk has an abundance, but our courier has the flu, as well, so I need to find an alternative, and I may need to call in medical help from Minsk, too."

He saw her lips press together. He knew she was checking the urge to comment on his lack of staffing.

Those lips…he couldn't get the kiss out of his mind.

He leaned forward and touched her shoulder. "Ginger, this past year has been more difficult than I'd ever imagined possible."

She didn't pretend to misunderstand. "I know."

"For you, too?"

She nodded as her gaze caressed his face.

"I hated that you felt I rejected you, when I wanted the opposite to be true."

She looked away. "Maybe we shouldn't talk about—"

"Because I love you, Ginger."

She stared at him, and, for once, didn't seem able to find a reply.

"I have for a long time," he said. "Probably years, though I was too bullheaded to admit it to myself. But then, you wouldn't know anything about bullheaded-ness, would you?"

She gave him a quick grin, then immediately sobered.

He took her hand. "Is it possible you may have some of those same feelings for me?"

Though she didn't pull her hand from his, he could feel her withdrawing. It amazed him how much that hurt.

"Obviously, I care for you, Ray," she said, her voice softer, her eyes sad.

"What is it that makes me think there's a 'but' coming?"

She took his hand in both of hers, raised it to her lips and kissed his knuckles. "Ray, you know my past. For too many years, I lived for myself and did what I wanted to do. I ignored God's call on my life, and wasted so much time when I could have been serving Him."

"You don't have to keep trying to earn your way to heaven, you know."

"I know that. Of course I do. But perhaps because I did turn my back on God for so much of my life, I can't let anything, or anyone, come between us now."

"That's the last thing I would do, and you know it."

"Ray, I've put out feelers at other mission boards for an overseas medical position."

"That doesn't surprise me, but why does it have to be overseas?"

"Because that's where my mission lies. You should be able to understand that. Your mission is Columbia. I've been saving my money, in case I can't find a paid position. I know I've been called to care for those less fortunate than I, and the huge majority of those people are in other countries and continents."

"But those aren't the only—"

"We're ready!"

Ginger released his hand, and she and Ray turned to see Helen coming through the kitchen between the children. Brittany's arm was tied expertly in a sling, the girls' clothing was dry, their hair pulled back in ponytails, and they each wore a ball cap.

"Helen, you're amazing," Ginger said.

"Let's go hiking now," Brittany said. "Okay? Lucy has Chuckles and umbrellas in her backpack."

Ginger stood up. "Let me change and get my boots on. I'll only be a couple of minutes." She gave Ray a final glance over her shoulder as she walked from the room, and he saw the regret in her eyes.

Ginger had only to sink her hiking boots into the Kauai mud to fall in love. "So this is Kauai in the winter. A person could get used to this."

A person could get used to having Ray Clyde around, too, but neither option was possible for her. She'd had her marriages, she'd lived that part of her life. It was over.

Why did it have to hurt so much?

"I want to wear the backpack," Brittany said. "I want to carry Chuckles."

"You can't," Lucy said. "You've been hurt, and you have to heal."

"Ray said I was fine."

"Ray said you had to wear a sling," Ginger reminded her. "Let Lucy and me take turns, and you walk and enjoy this beauty."

For sure, it continued to take Ginger's breath away. This mountainside resembled the luxuriant forests that surrounded Hideaway during the spring, summer and autumn months. Except, of course, for the palm trees, and the looming mountains, the sound of breakers hitting the rocky shoreline in the distance, and the smell of salt air.

Missouri had hills, no tall mountains.

The Napali Coastline was a rugged series of coastal mountains ending in sheer cliffs that dropped straight down into the sea. The area was uninhabited except for backpackers, and unreachable except by foot or by boat. She didn't know if this trail would eventually take them there, but later, when she got a chance to hike alone, she would check it out.

The children walked faster than Ginger had expected, and she paused at a turn in the trail to catch her breath. Unexpectedly, a view opened up before her, and she discovered an unobstructed vista of the ocean.

She gasped appreciatively. "Look, girls! Isn't it beautiful?"

Breathtaking. She could stand here and watch the shifting clouds and the colorful glow of the sinking sun for the rest of the night.

Ginger heard the catchy tune from her cell phone and dug it from her pocket. It was Taylor Jackson again.

"What's up this time," she asked. And why hadn't he called Larry instead? She was surprised the call had even come through.

"Just updating you about what we've got here, and I've got some questions that you'd probably be more likely to answer than anyone else."

"Why?"

"Because you spend the most time with the girls."

"And?"

"You know of anything Sandi Jameson might've had that Rick Fenrow would want? Did you find anything in her apartment after her death? Photos, documents, something you would have saved or placed in storage for the children?"

Ginger glanced at the girls and lowered her voice, stepping away a few feet. "Nothing that struck me as important. I'd say the police would have done a most thorough search the day…it happened. Want to tell me what's going on?"

"Wish I knew all the details," Taylor said. "I called the sheriff and deputy. With Blaze Farmer's help we went through Graham's house, because he knows the house better than the rest of us. Whoever broke in was thorough."

Ginger shook her head. "But what would he have

been looking for? You said pictures or documents. Of what?"

"That's what I wanted to know, so on a hunch, I called the prison where Fenrow had been held, And I learned some interesting things. I was put in touch with a friend, a former park ranger who I worked with at the Grand Canyon. He'd moved to Kansas and got into a ministry at this prison."

He knew Rick Fenrow from there?"

"That's right. A couple of weeks ago Fenrow was in a so-called accident in which an institutional-size refrigerator fell over and nearly crushed him. He was frantic when he called my friend. He said his cell mate was trying to kill him."

"Why would that be?" Ginger glanced down at the girls, then turned away from them and lowered her voice. "That's a serious accusation."

"It sounds legit," Taylor said. "Other reports backed him up. Fenrow is apparently in search of some sensitive information that Sandi was supposed to have had. In fact, the two of them had gathered that information, and Sandi was to compile it and hold it as incriminating evidence that would do major damage to a certain high-profile CEO's reputation, and possibly land him in prison. From what I understand of the situation, that information is at large, and this CEO is now aware of the evidence."

"So revenge might not be his only motive for following us," she said. "That doesn't make sense. Why would we have it here, of all places? We don't have anything that even resembles what he was looking for."

"How do you know?" Taylor asked.

"We packed essentials, not stray documents or pictures."

According to my friend, the last time Sandi talked to Fenrow, she told him that she was keeping the evidence for insurance to protect herself and her kids, and her kids would be helping her hide it."

Ginger gasped. "She involved..." Again, she glanced at the girls.

"That's right. She doesn't sound like a very nice person."

"You got that right." For Sandi to put Lucy and Brittany in danger by placing their names on Rick Fenrow's internal radar? Unconscionable!

"Let's hope Fenrow's found what he's looking for and didn't follow you there," Taylor said.

"I think he's already here, being held by the police. Larry, Graham and Willow are on their way to identify him."

There was a pause, the Taylor said, "Good! He skipped out of prison because he was convinced his life was forfeit. Apparently, his main motivation wasn't to inflict revenge on Willow again."

"Somehow that doesn't satisfy my curiosity."

"You might have what he's looking for, but it could be in a place you wouldn't expect. Are there any books the girls like to read that their mother gave them? She might have hidden something in a cover. Any keepsakes?"

"If she did have something, she could have left it in a safety deposit box at the bank," Ginger suggested.

"Tom's checking that angle now," Taylor said. "Let me know if you think of anything, and I'll call if I find anything out."

"Thanks." Ginger disconnected as she took a step closer to the edge, and without warning the moist earth crumbled beneath her feet. Her well-cushioned backside made intimate acquaintance with the thick undergrowth.

"Ouch!"

"Aunt Ginger, are you okay?" Lucy asked.

"I'm fine, my dear. Plenty of protection for me here." She patted a hip, then scrambled to her feet, making a pretense of allowing the children to help her, while trying not to trip over one of them.

"This place is dangerous," Lucy said. "Waves and crumbly trails." She cast a cautious look toward the wildly surging waves on the shore.

"But the forest is safe," Ginger promised. "Remember, no snakes, ticks, chiggers, poisonous spiders, or even mosquitoes up here."

"Coyotes?" Lucy took Ginger's left hand and tugged her on up the trail.

"Nope. Not that I know of."

Brittany grabbed her right hand. "Bears?"

"No bears," Ginger said, "except for good ol' Chuckles."

Ginger saw some delicious-looking blackberries growing on a vine less than a foot from the trail. Had her hands not been otherwise engaged, she'd have reached over and picked some.

Lucy's hand tightened on Ginger's. "Bad guys?"

"Sweetheart, remember Larry went to identify the man that—"

Lucy tugged hard on her hand and pointed into the trees to their left. "Aunt Ginger!"

Ginger looked. A man stood there, watching them from the trees.

TWENTY-TWO

Ray studied the mountainside from the living room window as he waited for another telephone connection to Kobrin, Belarus. Ginger and the children had disappeared from sight no more than five minutes ago—soon after the amusing vision of Ginger's fall in the mud.

He could barely think about anything except his last conversation with her. She must have been on target this morning when she suggested that he didn't have the heart of a foreign missionary. He couldn't understand why she felt such a strong urge to leave America, when there were so many in need within these borders.

So many in need. And he was one of them. He needed her in his life. Selfish of him to think that way, but right now he could focus on nothing else.

The call disconnected on him again, for the third time in the past fifteen minutes. Nothing seemed to work right today, least of all him. All he wanted was a good counterargument to convince Ginger to stay.

He put the receiver down, then on a whim picked it up and dialed the police in Poipu to see if Larry had arrived to identify their suspect.

The man he reached knew nothing about the capture. Once again, as Ray watched for a flash of color or movement on the mountainside, he waited until the operator could connect him to a supervisor who might know something.

It didn't happen. He gripped the receiver, controlling his frustration with difficulty. "Sir, are you telling me there was no suspect apprehended that matched the description of Rick Fenrow, a prison escapee that Larry Bager warned the force about earlier today?"

"I'm sorry, but we've found no suspect."

"Then is Larry Bager there yet? He received a call about an hour ago with that information, and he left our place here in Haena to drive to Poipu to identify the man being held."

"I doubt he's had time to get all the way to Poipu from Haena, so maybe that's the problem. Must be some misunderstanding."

"I'm not willing to settle for that," Ray snapped. "We've got an escaped prisoner who might well be on the island. We have women and children in our group, and we need protection." He gave their address and asked for a patrol car to come out.

The only misunderstanding Ray could see was that someone had called Larry about Rick Fenrow, and the information was false.

So who'd called Larry? And where was Fenrow if he hadn't, after all, been apprehended?

Ray decided it was best to get everyone inside the house. Something was up. A madman was on the loose.

Ginger didn't like the stranger's sunglasses. Who wore sunglasses when hiking in the forest shadows?

She didn't like the way he moved toward them, casual, yet watchful.

He had short blond hair and blond eyebrows, was slender and had a nice tan—or it appeared so in the diffused light of the setting sun.

"Fellow hikers, I see," he called to them, stepping down the steep mountainside through a thicket of vines. He wasn't on a trail. A pair of binoculars hung from a strap around his neck.

Lucy tugged on Ginger's hand. "Aunt Ginger, let's go back *now.*"

"No!" Brittany cried. "We haven't reached the top of the mountain."

"We'll come back later." Ginger drew the girls away as the man stepped close, her grip firm on a hand of each child. "Right now, I think I smell dinner grilling." She gave the man a nod, turned around and started back down the trail.

"Did you say dinner?" He slid down the final few feet of the steep bank and landed in front of them, as if by accident.

That was when she knew.

"Would there be enough for one more person at the table?" He held out his arms. "I'm about starved, and so thirsty. There are a lot of little streams on this mountain, but you know how the forest service always warns you not to drink unpurified water, even here in beautiful Hawaii."

"I have a bottle of water in my pack," Ginger said, though she didn't make a move for the pack. She didn't want to let go of either of the girls' hands. "We aren't far from the highway. Where did you leave your vehicle?"

"Down at Ke'e Beach. I started walking the Napali Coastline Trail and got lost." He shrugged and chuckled. "My wife always warns me not to go hiking unprepared."

She glanced at his ring finger. Sure enough, there was a band. But there was also a streak of more deeply tanned skin around the edges of his palm. As if he'd applied some of that artificial tan with that hand, and had failed to remove the stain completely. She wondered what else was artificial. The blond hair, perhaps? The eyebrows?

Lucy tugged at her again. "Come on, Aunt Ginger, they'll be waiting for us."

"Why don't you come with us?" Brittany invited the man. "I'm Brittany. What's your name?"

Ginger tried to step past him with the girls, but he blocked her with an awkward stumble that looked as if he were simply clumsy. He took a few steps backward, as if considering Brittany's invitation. As if he intended to fall into step with them and accompany them down the trail. But he didn't get out of their way, and he didn't turn his back on them.

It took all Ginger's control to continue to appear calm. *Oh, Lord, please help us.*

"My name's Gary Richter," he said. "Pleased to make

your acquaintance, Miss Brittany." He reached out as if to shake the child's left hand.

Ginger refused to release her, even though Brittany tried to tug from her grip.

"Where are you from, Mr. Richter?" Ginger asked.

He didn't reply. She couldn't see his eyes behind the dark glasses, but she sensed his muscles tensing. She knew this was Rick Fenrow and there would be no way to talk him into letting her and the girls leave.

"Lucy," she said, without looking away from the man. "Remember how proud I was of you for what you did today?"

"Yes." Lucy's voice held the tightness of fear.

"That's my girl." She stepped toward Rick Fenrow, at the same time forcing the girls to step behind her. As soon as she felt Lucy reach out to grab her sister's hand, Ginger released the girls and rushed at the man, bringing her elbows up, her arms protecting her face.

"Run, girls! Get away!" She brought her hiking boot down hard on Fenrow's instep, then jerked up with her knee.

He blocked her, grunting with pain as he caught her arms. Brittany screamed. Fenrow grabbed Ginger's throat with both hands.

She kicked him on the shin and tried to hit him in the solar plexus. He blocked, grunted again and stumbled forward.

From the side, she saw Lucy shove at him.

"No, Lucy, run! Now! Get—"

He grabbed Ginger's hair, jerked her head back and then grabbed her throat and squeezed with painful cruelty.

She choked, trying to scream, gagging. Praying.

"You kids better stop or I'll kill Aunt Ginger!" he shouted.

Ginger curled her arm forward, then shoved backward with her elbow. "Keep going, Lucy!"

The blow landed. The breath went out of him. His hold on her throat eased. Ginger hit him again, then shoved up and back with her fist. It connected with his nose. Once more, she jabbed with her elbow, then punched at his nose, and he stumbled back.

She wrenched away, fell to the ground, filled her hands with sandy dirt and rocks and slung the gravel into his face.

He cried out and spat, brushed at his face, spat again.

She picked up a thick fallen limb of a tree and smacked him over the head. The rotten limb broke in two. She tried to scream for help, but her throat wouldn't work.

She looked for the girls, and saw Lucy leading Brittany through a thicket above the road. They were going the wrong way, not back to the house, but up, where the killer could cut them off.

Fenrow came after Ginger, silent with fury, his face coated with mud. She tried to turn and run, but he kicked her feet from under her. She landed with a thud on her side.

His hands found her throat once again, and his fingers tightened until she couldn't breathe. He rammed her head against the ground, squeezed her throat even tighter, rammed her head again.

He showed no mercy.

The dark forest spun around her. The girls had to get away. They had to!

She couldn't breathe. The forest spun faster, then went black.

Lucy couldn't go down the mountain, so she ran up, dragging Brittany behind her through brush that scraped her arms and caught in her hair.

"Stay away from the mud," she whispered to Brittany. "That way he can't see where we went. Stay on the grass and leaves."

"Okay."

"Don't look back, and don't slow down. Aunt Ginger said for us to run."

And so they ran.

Brittany stumbled on some loose rocks and cried out, but Lucy pulled her on. They had to get away. That was a bad man. Lucy knew it, but didn't know how she knew. He didn't look like Rick Fenrow, but she kept thinking about hair in bottles.

Brittany tripped again. Lucy stopped and looked back. He hadn't followed them…yet. They were surrounded by bushes and tall grass, and the stickery plants Aunt Ginger had told them were blackberry briars.

"Where are we?" Brittany asked with a whine in her voice.

Lucy grabbed her and covered her mouth. "Be quiet," she whispered, pulling her sister deeper into the thick bushes. "Be careful not to get caught in the stickers. Maybe he won't find us here."

Brittany scrambled in behind her. She knew how

to be quiet. They both knew how to hide when someone dangerous was nearby. They were out of practice, but they knew.

TWENTY-THREE

Ray couldn't reach Larry, Graham or Willow on their cell phones, even from the landline. He tried Ginger's cell, and wasn't surprised when he got no answer. Probably no signal. Steve hadn't returned from the grocery store, so they had no vehicle. He found Preston on the roof deck, sprawled in one of the chairs, staring toward the sun as it disappeared past the horizon.

"I think we have a problem," Ray said.

Preston frowned up at him. "What's wrong?"

"The police never called Larry."

Chair legs scraped against wood as Preston rose slowly to his feet. "What do you mean? You think he lied about the call?"

"*Someone* might have called him, but the police told me it wasn't them. They don't have anyone in custody, and never did."

A shadow of fear darkened Preston's eyes. "Willow and Graham are with Larry. Do you think Fenrow might have made the call to get Larry away from the house?"

"Only if he knew how to contact us," Ray said.

Preston held his gaze. "If he saw us leave the hotel this morning, he could have been watching our cars all day. He could've tailed us here."

"Ginger's on the mountain trail with the girls," Ray said. "You try to reach Steve and get him back here ASAP."

"Since there's no cell reception, how could Fenrow have reached Larry?"

"Larry didn't say, but he probably called on a landline. It would be easy to find the phone number, since the owner's name is on the mailbox."

Preston followed Ray to the stairway. "I'll have Helen call the store and ask them to page Steve."

"Good. We need a car. I'll go find Ginger and the girls and get them back to the house."

"Is there anything we can use for a weapon?" Preston asked. "We're helpless here."

"Not for long. The police are aware of the situation, so I expect them soon. We can't panic. I could be jumping to conclusions, but I don't want to chance it."

"I'm checking inside for some kind of weapon, and I'll follow you up the trail."

Ray hurried back down the steps and ran to find Ginger and the girls.

Lucy crouched on her knees beside Brittany and tried to see through the briar stalks. All she heard was Brittany's soft, frightened breathing and the rush of wind in the trees. The wind was getting stronger, and the sun was almost down. Here in the shadows she could barely see Brittany's face.

Maybe Aunt Ginger had already beaten the man up and was looking for them. But if she was, she'd be calling for them. Best not to move or make noise until she heard Aunt Ginger's voice.

The man was Rick Fenrow. Lucy was sure of that now. She could close her eyes and see the shape of his nose and chin, the straight cheeks, flat and ugly. He was the man in the window.

She reached down and rubbed Brittany's head. It would be okay. It would all be okay. They had lots of people who loved them now, who wouldn't let anything happen to them. They didn't have that before, and that was why Mama died.

The wind raced through the trees, whistling, twisting, whirling. The storm.

Lucy had never been afraid of storms. She liked to watch the movement of the trees, hear the sound of thunder, like people clapping their hands far away. She liked to feel the first splatters of rain on her cheeks, and smell the air.

A thud startled her. There was a scrape of rocks nearby. Brittany caught her breath, and Lucy pressed her fingers over her sister's lips. *Be quiet.*

She peeked through the briars, and nearly screamed when she saw the man's legs, jeans dirty, tennis shoes brown instead of white.

"I see you," he called softly, and then he laughed.

Ray knew nothing could be worse than the terrifying images within his own mind as he ran up the trail. "Ginger!" he called, "where are you? Time to come down. Lucy? Brittany? Can you hear me?" The wind whipped his voice away. The trees seemed to lunge at him, dipping and swirling.

He could no longer see the house through the trees, as he had followed the curve of the trail up and around the northern slope of the mountain. From where he stood, he saw that the trail followed the edge of the mountain up a series of switchbacks.

Ginger would never have taken the girls over anything that looked dangerous.

"Ginger!" Where had they gone? Maybe another trail branched away from the main one, and they had explored it. Whichever way Ginger had taken them, she should be on her way back by now...in fact, he should have run into the three of them long before now.

No time to panic. He needed to keep looking. They couldn't have—

He caught sight of a bright blue patch up ahead, at the edge of the first switchback. It was the color of Ginger's backpack.

"Ginger!"

It didn't move.

He ran.

Lucy pressed her fingers against Brittany's lips. *Don't speak. He may not really see us. Maybe he's faking.*

"You might as well come out," the man said. "I'm not going to hurt you." He sounded calm. Normal.

Lucy knew he wasn't normal. She wished she was as big and strong as Graham, then she wouldn't have to be afraid.

"I didn't come here to hurt you," the man said.

She gritted her teeth. He was a liar. He *had* hurt Aunt Ginger.

Brittany started to cry softly, and Lucy tapped her lips again, rubbing her head. *Be quiet. It's okay. I'm here.*

"I need something from you girls, and I can't let you go until I get it." His voice carried loudly over the wind, as if he didn't know for sure that they were crouched nearly at his feet.

She peered up at his hands. She couldn't see farther, because of the thickness of the bushes. He didn't have a gun in his hand. Maybe if they ran they could get away. Maybe Brittany could get away.

"You see, I knew your mother. She and I were friends, and we collected some information about an evil person who was hurting a lot of other people."

Lucy lowered her mouth close to Brittany's ear. "Don't listen to him," she whispered very softly. "He's—"

"Your mother knew who those people were, and she had some pictures that were mine. I was going to turn them in to the police." He took another step closer to them. Brittany tensed. Lucy pressed her down. *Don't move.*

"She told me you were helping her hide the pictures." *No way!*

"You want the police to get the people who really killed your mother, don't you? They got the wrong person the first time."

The wind stirred the briars. One poked Lucy in the shoulder. She gritted her teeth at the pain.

Brittany leaned closer to Lucy, and Lucy whispered, "Get ready to run when I tell you to. Go down the road."

Brittany shook her head.

Lucy tapped her hard on the shoulder. "Do it."

A sound rose over the whistle of wind, and it grew louder. It was a siren somewhere below them.

The man took a step closer. He pushed some of the briars aside, then jerked his hand back with a grunt. "We're out of time. You're coming with me now!"

Lucy shoved Brittany. "Go! Get away!"

The hand came down on Lucy's backpack. She screamed.

"Now! Hurry!" she cried, then turned and bit the man as hard as she could.

Ray's lungs burned, sweat dripping from his face as he took the final curve and saw that the blue swathe of color was, indeed, Ginger's backpack. Ginger still wore it.

She lay collapsed at the edge of the trail. *No, please no. This can't be happening!*

She lay half on her side, and shadows fell over her face. Purple shadows, unnatural in the twilight.

"Ginger!" He ran and fell to his knees beside her. Those shadows were made of blood and dirt...and blue smudges that looked like bruises. Her shirt was ripped, her throat bruised and swollen.

"Ginger, come on, wake up. Don't do this to me!"

He gently grasped her shoulders. "Ginger?" He bent low over her face, but could hear nothing over the wail of the wind and a siren in the distance.

He grasped her jaw and opened her mouth. When he bent close, he could feel the warm moisture of her breath.

She was breathing. He pressed his hand to the side

of her face, then reached for her carotid artery to see if she had a pulse. "Ginger, please. Wake up."

Airway good. Breathing good. Circulation good. Her neck looked as if she'd been choked. Her face looked purple in places, as if someone had beaten her...or as if vessels had ruptured from the choking.

He looked around them. "Lucy! Brittany!"

The siren grew louder. He palpated Ginger's neck for possible damage, felt her head for signs of concussion, then looked up the side of the mountain.

What had happened here? Ginger would never have tried anything dangerous with the children, so these injuries couldn't be from a fall.

Someone must have found them here and attacked... Ginger had fought. But *where* were the children now?

The wind eased for a few seconds, and the siren died. That was when he heard the scream.

TWENTY-FOUR

The man stumbled backward with an angry grunt, then came at Lucy again. He grabbed the pack on her back.

She raised her arms and slipped out of the straps. "Run, just run!" she screamed at Brittany. She stumbled, fell to her knees and felt his hand in her hair. She screamed and ran through a break in the thicket.

He grunted with pain. Probably caught in the brambles that had scratched her.

She left him behind holding the pack with Chuckles and three umbrellas.

Rain splashed her and wind flicked her hair into her face as she ran up the mountain. She didn't dare look back, but she heard him coming behind her, getting closer.

Lucy was a fast runner. She always won races in school, but she couldn't run faster than a grown-up. He was going to catch her. Even as the rain splashed down like a waterfall, and the wind blew so hard it shoved her forward, it wouldn't slow him down.

She stumbled in a slick spot and her feet flew out from under her. She landed hard on the ground. Lightning flashed, and to her horror, as Rick Fenrow grabbed her shirt and jerked her up, she saw the white foam of the ocean waves below, heard the pounding of the water as it crashed against the shore, and saw the jagged white line of the cliffs. They were on top of the cliffs!

She turned to look up at Rick Fenrow, and in another lightning flash she saw the whiteness of his teeth as he smiled.

He jerked her forward. "You don't have anywhere else to go, kid. Tell me where your mother hid those pictures."

"But I don't know what you're talking about!" she cried. How could he think she would know about that? She was a kid. Just a kid.

Rain blinded her, and his hands slipped down her arms. He shoved her out toward the cliff, laughing. "You want to take a swim? It's a jump, but you can do it, can't you?"

"No!" she screamed.

"Then you can tell me what your mother gave you."

"I don't know anything!"

He shook her. "Think! What did your mother give you before she died? Did she give you a book, or a toy, something for school?"

"No! Why don't you listen? I don't know what you're talking about!"

Even as she struggled with him, she saw a dot of light behind him. Another one joined it. Flashlights?

It wasn't lightning.

She saw people running up the mountain, shadows in the storm.

She stopped struggling. "You killed my mother."

"No, I didn't. Why would I have killed her? She had

something I needed. She told me her kids had it, and then she laughed at me. I hit her, but I didn't kill her. That would have been stupid."

"Then who killed her?"

"We'll find that out when we get those pictures."

Lucy wanted to cry. She didn't have any pictures.

A streak of light flicked through the rain, and Rick Fenrow spun around, jerking Lucy against him. "Who's there?"

"Let her go, Fenrow."

Lucy gasped. "Ray!"

Fenrow's hands tightened on Lucy's arm. "Now you're being silly," he called back. "You know I can't do that. She's not getting away alive if you come closer. You might say this little girl's my death benefit. If you don't leave me alone, she dies."

Lucy closed her eyes tight. Mama used to threaten to kill them, especially Lucy, when Mama needed a fix and couldn't get one. Later, she always cried and said she didn't mean it. Mama always said and did things she didn't mean when she was mad.

If he didn't kill Mama, then he won't kill me.

"You have the wrong person," Fenrow yelled at the others. "I didn't—"

Someone slammed into them from the side. Lucy fell hard and rolled out of Fenrow's reach, to the edge of the slick rock. Her foot slid over the edge and she screamed.

The wind whipped rain into her face, blinding her. She heard scuffling and grunting nearby. A foot shoved into her side, forcing her closer to the edge of the rock.

She screamed again.

Lightning flashed, and she saw someone leaning over her.

"I've got you, Lucy. Hold on." Graham. Strong arms lifted her and wrapped her in safety.

She buried her face against his shoulder.

"I've got you," he said. "It's okay now."

She wrapped her arms around his neck and held on tight. "Daddy?"

"I'm here."

"Brittany's out in the—"

"She's safe now."

"How did you get back?"

"We got worried, and I called the police when we could get a connection on the cell phone. We tried calling you at the house, but couldn't reach you. We raced back here as fast as we could come."

There was a sound of a gunshot behind them; a scream echoed through the heavy air. The scuffling stopped.

A moment later, Larry Bager's voice reached them through the darkness. "I got him. It's okay. It's all over."

Ray started back down the mountain. The storm had lightened, and the mountain was now crawling with police. He knew the girls were safe—Brittany had met them as she ran screaming down the mountain, streaked with blood from the briar patch. Willow was with her now. Graham had Lucy.

He knew, also, that an ambulance had been called, and that Steve and Helen Courtney were with Ginger, but Ray needed to be there, to see that she was okay.

Before he could reach the trail, however, Preston came running back up the mountain.

"I need your help, Ray."

"With what? I want to make sure Ginger—"

"Ginger's awake. I talked to Helen. We got a call from Taylor Jackson in Hideaway before I left the house. Fenrow isn't our only problem. Do you know where Lucy left her backpack?"

"She told us she dropped it as she was trying to get away from—"

Preston slapped him on the arm, then pointed along the hillside. "There."

Though the power of the storm had let up, lightning continued to flicker enough to give them a twilight view of a small thicket of bushes about thirty feet away…and a man bending over something on the ground.

"That's Larry," Ray said. "Looks like he's got things under control."

"That's what I'm worried about." Preston started in that direction. "Come with me."

Ray didn't want to waste time getting to Ginger, even if she *was* awake. He wanted to see her, touch her, make sure everything was working.

But something was up. Preston wasn't one to panic.

Preston shone the wide beam of his flashlight on Larry's back. "What'cha got there, Larry?"

No reply. Larry continued to work over something in front of him.

Preston and Ray drew closer.

Larry turned and glared into the light. "Would you turn that thing off?"

"I don't think so." Preston stepped up to him and shone the light on the small backpack Lucy had been carrying. The bear, Chuckles, lay in Larry's lap. "How sweet," Preston said. "I didn't know he meant that much to you."

"Yeah, well, he means a lot to Brittany. I'm sure she's asking for him."

"Really?" Preston reached down and took the bear from Larry's hands. "I'm on my way down. I'll just—"

Larry tried to grab it back, but Preston was faster. "Funny thing, Larry. I got to thinking this afternoon about how Brittany always talked about how Chuckles stopped laughing when their mother died. Then we got word from some friends at home about some evidence Fenrow was supposed to be searching for. Funny you didn't know anything about that."

"I don't know what you're talking about." Larry rose slowly to his feet.

"I think you do," Preston said. "I think you've been telling us only what you needed us to know to get us to cooperate with you. We couldn't leave this island to evade Fenrow, because you wanted to nab him yourself if you could. You didn't have to kill him, Larry."

Preston turned the bear over and held its back to the light. A square of fur was missing, and the inner workings of the battery mechanism was visible. "Tell us where you put the—"

Larry pivoted and charged up the hill. Preston dropped the bear and started after him.

"Watch him!" Ray called. "He's still got the gun!"

Preston ignored Ray and tackled Larry. Ray shouted

for the police, then lunged for the two men wrestling in the mud.

The gun went off, its blast echoing across the cliffs with the sound of returning thunder.

Ginger stared at the hideous monster in the mirror. The whites of both her eyes were mottled with bright red from burst capillaries. Her forehead and temples were bandaged, her face was purple-blue, with a deeper bruise on her right cheek. Her neck had dark fingerprints from Fenrow's hands.

She returned to her hospital bed. Before Ginger had left Missouri, Mrs. Engle had promised her that Hawaii would give her a whole new understanding of the word *colorful*. Well, she definitely had a new understanding of it.

She'd received word from Willow a few minutes ago that Lucy and Brittany had both been checked through the E.R. and were doing fine, with minimal scratches and bruises from the night's drama. Ginger hoped their emotional state would fare as well.

Someone knocked at the closed door, and Ginger turned her back to it, facing the window. She didn't want anyone to see her face.

"Ginger?" It was Ray.

"I'm here." Her voice was gravelly and hoarse. She even sounded like a monster.

She heard his quick footsteps to her bedside, felt his hand on her shoulder. "I hear you're doing better," he said. "I'd like to see them monitor you a little more closely, though."

"I'm fine," she rasped.

"Your throat took quite a beating, and I'm concerned about head injury. You were out for quite some time."

"They're doing frequent neuro checks," she assured him.

He stepped around the foot of the bed, and she saw him wince when he caught sight of her face. She wanted to cover her head with the sheet.

"It looks better than it did," he said.

"You're all charm."

"The girls want to make sure you're okay."

"You can tell them I'm dancing a jig in here." She knew her sarcasm lost much of its sting with the hoarseness. "Don't let them come in and see for themselves."

Ray sat on the edge of the bed and took her hand. "You're bound to be a little grumpy after what you've been through."

She ignored the gibe. "Do the police have Fenrow in custody? Please tell me this nightmare is over." She suddenly recalled that the last time she'd spoken of a nightmare, it had been this morning—which felt like a decade ago. Her comment then had been in reference to Ray's presence on the island.

"If you hadn't been here, Ray…" She closed her eyes. "I can't bear to imagine what might have happened to us."

He didn't reply. She noticed he hadn't replied to her question about Rick Fenrow, either.

"What are you trying to protect me from this time?" She opened her eyes again, and looked at him.

He met her gaze. "Larry shot Fenrow."

She caught her breath. "When? No one told me that. What happened?"

"I believe it took place about the time they loaded you into the ambulance. Fenrow got desperate and tried to hold Lucy hostage. It didn't work out as he'd planned."

Sudden tears filled Ginger's eyes. *Oh, Lucy. My little sweetheart. What kinds of dreams will you have now?*

"Is he dead?" she asked.

Ray squeezed her shoulder. "Yes."

Ginger wasn't so horrified by his death as she was by the sense of relief she felt at the news. What had happened to her compassion? That man was lost for eternity. What agony must he be suffering?

And yet, he had chosen his own fate by the decisions he'd made in life. That didn't make the tragedy any more palatable, but Ginger reminded herself she had a bad tendency to take the responsibility of the world on her shoulders.

"Did Lucy see it?" she finally asked, her voice now hoarse with tears.

"Graham was holding her when the shot was fired," Ray said. "She didn't see anything. She only knew that the people who loved her most in the world were there for her when she needed them."

"And Brittany?"

"Safe in her mother's arms."

Ginger was struggling to recover from the shock when Graham walked in. He was alone. That meant he, too, had deemed it wise not to let the girls see her in her present condition.

"You heard about Larry and Rick?" Graham asked her.

Ginger nodded. She was getting tired, and her head hurt.

"Then there was an accident when Preston jumped Larry," Graham said.

Ginger looked at him in confusion. "What? Why would Preston jump Larry?"

"You know the evidence Rick had been looking for, that Taylor Jackson told you about?" Ray asked.

"Yes, he called me about it when we were on the trail."

"That evidence turned out to be a memory card with photos and documents that Sandi and Rick had taken of Larry's employer."

Ginger looked at her brother. "You're Larry's employer."

"Apparently, I was only one of them."

She felt as if she'd stepped into someone else's nightmare for once. "I'm missing something here."

"Larry wasn't working for us, Ginger. His real employer is the head of a crime cartel that controls holdings all across the Midwest. Rick and Sandi had collected photos and documents that would incriminate Larry's employer."

"Larry *used* us?" Ginger exclaimed. "Ray, didn't I tell you I felt like bait in a trap?"

"Yes, and I disagreed. I'm sorry."

"Larry is dead, too," Graham said. "He and Preston were struggling for the gun, and it went off. It hit Larry in the chest."

Ginger suddenly couldn't breathe. The shock of this fresh news chilled her to the bone.

"Larry had been trying to get the memory card of data from Chuckles, where Sandi had hidden it last year," Ray said.

Ginger shook her head. "That's why the bear didn't laugh. Would someone mind telling me how Larry managed to find his way into our confidence in the first place?"

"That's my fault," Graham said. "Larry first approached me at a town meeting last year, where he gave me his business card. Then he followed up a few weeks later with a visit to the clinic. He seemed polished and professional."

"Of course," Ginger said. "He was a cop for many years. He knew how to play it."

"I've discovered he was doing surveillance on some people moving into my apartment complex," Graham said.

"Rick and Sandi, of course," Ginger said.

"Then when Rick set fire to Preston's cabin, and it became obvious he was stalking Willow, Larry was there, waiting for me to contact him," Graham said.

"So Larry was dirty for years," Ray said.

"That's right," Graham told him. "He's good, because none of his coworkers ever guessed he was working both sides. Since long before retiring from the force, he'd been the go-to guy for a dirty corporate CEO who couldn't afford to be identified or his whole regime would fall."

"Where did Rick fit in with this?" Ray asked.

"Rick's father was set up, and though he was dirty, Rick was convinced he took the fall for a lot of things he didn't do. Rick was desperate to prove his father's innocence and get him out of jail. Later, Rick wanted the evidence to prove Larry wasn't an upstanding P.I."

Ginger closed her eyes, suddenly feeling exhausted. Her heart ached more than her head. She was more than ready for this trip to end.

"When can we go home?" she asked.

TWENTY-FIVE

Ginger sat on the back deck of her cozy, two-bedroom condo shadowed by a tree-lined cliff, complete with a trickling waterfall, chattering squirrels and two white-tailed deer that peered at her between the white branches of leafless sycamore trees.

It was unseasonably warm for the first week of February, and Ginger had enjoyed sunshine and temperatures in the sixties for the past four days. Why go to Hawaii when a person could get this wonderful weather literally in her own backyard?

To the front of the condo, out Ginger's living room window, there was a view of Lake Taneycomo, and in the distance, Branson Landing, one of the most exclusive new shopping centers in the four-state area.

She was within a ten-minute drive of just about anything she could possibly want to buy. She'd made new friends at a Bible study sponsored by a newly established church in the area. She kept busy.

She got to see Lucy and Brittany at least twice a week—and had discovered yesterday she was to be an aunt again. Even more exciting, this morning her oldest son, Phillip, had called from St. Louis to tell her she would be a grandmother for the first time.

How much better did life get? What a wonderfully blessed woman she was.

So why didn't she feel grateful? Why did she, in fact, feel like crying?

She knew some of her problem stemmed from the excitement of early January. She still had some bruises on her face and neck, though the lingering chartreuse was nearly gone. She knew Lucy and Brittany continued to struggle with disillusionment about Larry Bager's part in the Rick Fenrow fiasco, though they basked in the love of their new parents.

What they didn't know, and wouldn't for years to come, was that recent evidence pointed to the probability that Larry, and not Rick, had actually been the one who'd killed Sandi. After going back over all Rick's earlier testimony, and speaking to eyewitnesses that placed Larry in the vicinity of Sandi Jameson's apartment on the morning of her murder, the authorities had deduced that Larry Bager had placed the final blow that killed Sandi.

Rick Fenrow may have attempted to use force to get her to tell him where the photographs were, but Larry had most likely done the final deed.

A man they had trusted with their lives had been a killer.

Good had come from these revelations. Larry's employer no longer controlled the empire of a wealthy company. The evidence that had been hidden in the stuffed bear, Chuckles, was bringing down a whole infrastructure of evil.

Ginger closed her eyes and thanked God for protecting them, and especially the children.

She'd heard no word about her latest résumé for a missions opportunity in Chernobyl, and held little hope that she would hear anything this week. In fact, now that she knew about her grandchild, she couldn't deny some hesitation about future prospects.

The telephone rang inside. Its shrill sound carried through the glass doors.

She tried to ignore it, listening, instead, to the trickle of water down the side of the cliff, and the call of a mourning dove in the bare-branched dogwood tree in the yard.

The phone stopped ringing, and she heard her own voice recite its spiel on the answering machine. Then a dial tone. The call was a hang-up.

Fine. If whoever it was didn't care enough to leave a message, then it was okay if she didn't answer.

Two seconds later came a familiar tune, the one she'd chosen for her cell phone because it always made her want to dance. Today she wanted to cover her head with a pillow and wish the world away. The tune irritated her.

With great reluctance, as if lifting a heavy weight, she pulled herself from the deck chair and slid open the glass door. The tune stopped before she could reach the cell on her kitchen counter. But it began its tune again almost immediately.

She yanked it up and flipped it open. The caller number was blocked. "Yes!"

"Are you home?"

She paused, suddenly flustered. "Ray?"

"That's right. Are you home?"

"Yes, but—"

The doorbell rang.

"Don't you think you'd better answer that?" he asked.

In spite of every inner warning, she felt a smile try to spread across her face. "Ray Clyde, is that you downstairs?" The front door to her condo was at the bottom of a carpeted staircase. She didn't get a lot of company.

"Nope."

"Oh." She rushed to the living room, where she could barely peer out the front window and see who was standing there. It was a woman she didn't recognize. Probably looking for the renter in the downstairs unit. That happened a lot.

"Ginger? You still there?" Ray asked.

"Can I call you back? Looks like someone needing directions."

"I can hold."

Ginger grimaced. "I'll call you right back." She snapped the phone shut, and as her toes sank into the thick carpet on the stairs, she couldn't help wondering why she and Ray always seemed to be at odds. It was as if they were born to disagree about practically everything.

And she really didn't want it to be that way.

She opened the door to find the lost lady smiling, holding a huge basket of tropical goodies—a coconut, a pineapple, passion fruit and guava, with packets of coffees grown in Kauai, and a beautiful, huge red poinsettia centerpiece. And a teddy bear with a Hawaiian grass skirt.

"Uh." Ginger gaped at the smiling woman. "Hello. This is 170B, not A. Are you sure you have the right place?"

The lady, blond and petite and wearing a Realtor badge on her jacket that identified her as Jan, laughed. "You know a hunk named Ray Clyde? Because if you refuse this gift from a man like that, I'd be glad to take him off your hands."

"Ray sent this?"

"Yes, and I'd say he went to quite a bit of trouble to do it. We don't have a lot of guava in Missouri. Or passion fruit, for that matter."

Ginger thanked the woman and took the basket, then once more looked around outside. Could he be lurking in the shadows to see what her reaction would be? How could the woman know he was a hunk if she hadn't actually laid eyes on him?

After three weeks of not hearing a word from him, now he was sending her fruit and flower baskets?

Still…she took the bounty upstairs and set it on the kitchen table, then searched for a card. There was none. She did, however, find chocolate candy. Dark chocolate with coconut, pineapple and macadamia nuts.

She was sinking her teeth into a corner of the rich, decadent bar when her cell phone rang again. She reached for it and flipped it open. "Thank you," she said with a slightly full mouth.

"You're really speaking to me?" he asked.

She chewed and swallowed. "Why wouldn't I?"

There was a pause, then, "You haven't heard from Future Investments?"

She caught her breath and nearly choked on a maca-damia nut. Oh, no. What had he done now? "Not in the past few days." Future Investments was the mission organization that sent food and medical care into some of the most politically dangerous countries in the world. It was one of the groups with whom she had applied for a position. "Ray Clyde—"

"I told them the truth when they asked for a recommendation."

She slowly folded the wrapping back over the candy and put it away. "Mind telling me what that truth was?"

"That you are as honest as the day is long."

All right! "You should be arrested for heavy-handed clichés."

"And that you couldn't keep your mouth shut about sensitive information."

Ray Clyde was going to die. "Ever cracked a coconut?" she snapped.

"Uh, I don't see what a coconut has to do—"

"Your head would work. I've got the—"

"Now, Ginger, hold on. I have another idea you might want to hear before you go busting heads."

"I'm not interested in—"

The doorbell rang again. Ginger flipped the cell phone shut and laid it on the counter.

Ray braced himself for the door to open. He'd done it again, and he wasn't sorry. Ginger didn't need to be in another dangerous situation. He'd simply told the truth. Her mouth could get her killed.

The door flew back, nearly hitting the wall behind it. Ginger's face was flushed, her eyes blazing. She looked as if she'd lost more weight in the past three weeks.

She looked tired. And angry, of course. It wouldn't

do to mention his observations aloud at this moment. At least the bruises were almost gone, though he had a feeling she didn't want to hear that, either.

Her eyes told him he really wouldn't have to say much to hang himself. "You told them *what?*"

"The truth." He kept his voice calm, and tried to infuse it with all the tenderness he felt for her. "I'm not going to lie, even for you. Especially not for you, since you do have that bad tendency to get yourself into trouble in certain situations, and I'm not going to contribute to—"

"Well, why don't you tell me exactly what it is you think I'm qualified to do, since I have such a tendency to put myself in danger."

"I have a perfect—"

"No, wait, you obviously don't think I have a brain in my head when it comes to dealing with people, so—"

"You know better. I have complete faith—"

"And traveling is obviously out." She turned to lead the way up the stairs. "Since I'm likely to jump-start a third world war if I even set foot in a foreign country."

"I need you in Columbia."

Her steps faltered, her momentum slowed. She reached out and grasped the banister, then continued up the steps without acknowledging what he said. Was it his imagination, or were her shoulders not quite as stiff, her movements not quite as jerky?

He followed her. "I realize Columbia, Missouri, is not a foreign country, but there are children in our own state who have been abandoned, who have nothing, and who need someone to take care of them. Lots of children."

She turned and looked down at him. Her warm brown eyes no longer blazed, but they mirrored confusion. "You're telling me to start an orphanage in Columbia?"

"I'm…no. I'm telling you I need…I'm offering you a job."

She blinked. "You think you can keep me out of trouble if I work for you in your practice?"

"Actually, it's a·two-part offer, but I'll get to the rest later."

Her eyes narrowed, and she put her hands on her hips. "I think you'd better explain what you're talking about. I've had enough of your word games today."

He swallowed. *Ray Clyde, there's no doubt you have a definite way with women. A bad way.* "Okay, it's like this. I've loved you for years, Ginger, you know that."

"Old news. I've given it a lot of thought, and realized that there are all kinds of love, Ray. Friends love each other. Even some *enemies* love each other, which is sick, but the Bible does say to love your enemy. Are you sure you aren't talking about that kind of love?"

"Never in my life have I thought of you as my enemy."

"Why don't I believe you?"

He took her hand, held it up, rubbed the back of it with his fingers. "It felt like the stab of a knife every time you left to go back to Belarus, but I made sure you always went back, because that was where your heart was."

She swallowed. "We're covering old ground here," she said, but her voice had softened.

He barely concealed his frustration. How could one woman be so bullheaded and obstinate?

And yet, her determination was one of the things he

loved about her. "I know you have a lot to offer," he said. "Your life as a missionary hasn't ended, and neither has your career with GlobeMed."

"GlobeMed is an *international* mission board."

"Sure it is," he said, "but that doesn't preclude us from having a mission in our own state. There's a great need for another children's home, and the funding has come through. I'm looking for someone who can be the director."

Her eyebrows raised. "And that would be...?"

"You."

For once, she appeared speechless. He pressed the initiative. "You would be the best person for the position, Ginger. Your heart is always softest when it comes to children."

She studied him closely. "You're serious?"

"Totally."

Her expression lightened further. "You're offering me the job?"

"That's what I'm doing, and as with your position in Belarus, you would be paid a salary. You wouldn't have to campaign for your support. We need you there, Ginger."

Her eyes—those beautiful eyes—widened. He had her. He knew it, and it was all he could do not to smile in triumph.

She withdrew her hand from his and turned away from him. "I'll have to think about it."

He gritted his teeth. She was toying with him, but he knew how to handle her now. "Then think about this, as well. From time to time, you may also be asked to travel out of country to help establish other children's homes."

She turned back. Grudging interest sparked in her eyes.

"I know how much you love to travel," he said.

"Is that the second part of the deal you mentioned?"

"Uh, no, that isn't it." He swallowed.

"Is this why you drove all the way here from Columbia?" she asked, sinking, at last, onto the sofa, and gesturing for him to join her. "To offer me a job? The telephone's a lot more convenient."

He didn't move. For the moment, he couldn't even think straight, much less focus on the effort it would take to decide where to sit—whether to light right beside her, or take the recliner across from her, or sit on the floor and babble like an idiot.

She frowned and cocked her head. "Ray?"

He cleared his throat. "This directorship is an important position."

"So?"

"I thought I might have some convincing to do, since you and I seldom see eye to eye about anything, and this job would mean spending a lot more time with me."

"If I were to take the job, that wouldn't be a problem."

"We might not always agree about the way things should be done."

She shook her head. "That's supposed to be news to me? Why did you drive all the way here to offer me a job?"

He sat down beside her then. "Because the second part of the deal is a lot more important, and it wasn't something I could talk to you about over the telephone."

"This is the second part of the job offer?"

He shrugged. "I think I might have said that wrong. It isn't exactly…what I mean to say is, there's a little more to it than…"

She leaned forward. "Why, Ray Clyde, I think you're blushing."

"I might be."

She rested her elbows on her knees. "You know, it's amazing that a man as fearless as you, who has no trouble talking about anything else, or proposing anything else, is afraid to propose marriage."

He stared into her eyes. Her face was so close it would be easy to lean forward and kiss her. "I'm a coward at heart."

"I've been afraid, too," she said, lifting a hand to touch his cheek. "But my biggest fear has been that I wouldn't see you again."

He swallowed, catching the scent of plumeria. She'd purchased a bottle of that perfume in Kauai. "So does this mean you'll marry me?"

Her eyes once more filled with laughter. She nodded. "It's the only way you'll get me to Columbia." She leaned closer and touched her lips to his, so lightly it almost tickled.

Before she could change her mind and back away, he caught her in his arms, pressing his lips to her chin, her cheek, her forehead as he held her close. "Did I mention that I love you?"

Her laughter filled the room and echoed in his heart. For the first time in many years, everything in his world felt right.

* * * * *

Look for A Hideaway Home
by Hannah Alexander,
available in early 2008 from the exciting new
Love Inspired Historical line.
And watch for Hannah Alexander's next
single title Hideaway book
available in January 2008 from Steeple Hill.

Dear Reader,

As you can imagine, we had a lot of fun researching this book in Hawaii. We love Kauai and are fascinated by the winter beauty, so different from ours here in the Ozarks. God's great, creative genius is obvious, with fruits of all kinds growing wild in the forests, ready for the picking. We did manage to get lost in the forest during our research trip, and discovered firsthand how easy it would be for a stalker to hide behind trees, shrubs and among the people.

Much as we love the physical exploration of our settings, we find that the study of the human heart is even more fascinating. When someone as emotionally healthy and proactive as Ginger Carpenter could hold a grudge for many months against someone she trusted and cared about for years, is it any wonder that Rick Fenrow could hold a grudge against Willow, coming, as he did, from a very dysfunctional background? But that doesn't excuse his actions, and he must pay the consequences for those actions.

Ginger, Ray, Graham, Willow, Steve and Helen all made choices and now must reap what they sowed. Ginger suffered with the pain of bitterness when she didn't forgive Ray, and Ray suffered the loss of her friendship when he didn't tell her the truth immediately and treat her as a mature adult. Steve and Helen inspired mistrust when they neglected to tell the group about their relationship with the girls in the first place. Graham and Willow risked a damaged relationship with Ginger when they kept the truth from her about Ray's part in the wedding trip.

Let us all strive to be more honest with one another and lovingly accept one another's faults, forgiving one another in our hearts as we try to live with authenticity.

With love,

Hannah Alexander

QUESTIONS FOR DISCUSSION

1. In an attempt to spare Ginger's feelings, Ray withholds important information that ends up damaging his relationship with her. How do you think both Ray and Ginger could have handled this situation better? Have you ever been in a similar situation?

2. Grant, Willow and Preston all agree to withhold information from Ginger in order to get her to go with them to Hawaii. Were they right in doing this (i.e., did the ends justify the means), especially since Ray and Ginger did get back together? What advice would you give them to handle the situation more appropriately?

3. Steve and Helen had ulterior motives for agreeing to be the wedding planners for Grant and Willow. Do you think they should have been more honest about why they wanted to go? How would you have handled the situation differently?

4. Several of the characters in *Death Benefits* withhold the truth from others, thinking they have noble reasons for doing so. Is it ever right to keep the truth from someone? Can you give an example? Can you give a biblical example? Have you ever done this? If so, why? Was anyone ever angry with you when they found out the truth? Would you do it differently if you had the chance?

5. Which do you feel is the stronger motivator: fear or revenge? Why is love superior to both? Can you give examples?

6. Would you take your family with you on your honeymoon if you were in Grant and Willow's situation? Why or why not?

7. Lucy has had to grow up quickly due to her mother's instability and drug dependency. What disadvantages will Lucy face with this premature maturity? What possible advantages do you think she might find from these qualities she's learned?

8. Earlier in the year, Ray was forced to remove Ginger from potential danger on the mission field and did not give her the real reason for this removal. This action damaged their friendship for many months. Knowing his reasons, what would you have done in the same situation?

9. When talking to Preston about his relationship with Sheila, Ginger uses the analogy of opening a cellophane bag of potato chips or salad greens with gentleness versus force. Can you share instances in your own life when you used gentleness instead of force with good results? Or vice versa?

10. What consequences might Ginger and Ray suffer in their future because of the long months of misunderstanding between them? Have you ever had a similar experience in your life? What consequences have you suffered?

REQUEST YOUR FREE BOOKS!

2 FREE RIVETING INSPIRATIONAL NOVELS
PLUS 2 FREE MYSTERY GIFTS

Love Inspired®
SUSPENSE

YES! Please send me 2 FREE Love Inspired® Suspense novels and my 2 FREE mystery gifts. After receiving them, if I don't wish to receive any more books, I can return the shipping statement marked "cancel." If I don't cancel, I will receive 4 brand-new novels every month and be billed just $3.99 per book in the U.S. or $4.74 per book in Canada, plus 25¢ shipping and handling per book and applicable taxes, if any*. That's a savings of 20% off the cover price! I understand that accepting the 2 free books and gifts places me under no obligation to buy anything. I can always return a shipment and cancel at any time. Even if I never buy another book from Steeple Hill, the two free books and gifts are mine to keep forever.

123 IDN EL5H   323 IDN ELQH

_____
Name   (PLEASE PRINT)

_____
Address   Apt. #

_____
City   State/Prov.   Zip/Postal Code

_____
Signature (if under 18, a parent or guardian must sign)

Order online at www.LoveInspiredSuspense.com

Or mail to Steeple Hill Reader Service™:

IN U.S.A.: P.O. Box 1867, Buffalo, NY 14240-1867
IN CANADA: P.O. Box 609, Fort Erie, Ontario L2A 5X3

Not valid to current Love Inspired Suspense subscribers.

Want to try two free books from another series?
Call 1-800-873-8635 or visit www.morefreebooks.com

* Terms and prices subject to change without notice. NY residents add applicable sales tax. Canadian residents will be charged applicable provincial taxes and GST. This offer is limited to one order per household. All orders subject to approval. Credit or debit balances in a customer's account(s) may be offset by any other outstanding balance owed by or to the customer. Please allow 4 to 6 weeks for delivery.

Your Privacy: Steeple Hill is committed to protecting your privacy. Our Privacy Policy is available online at www.eHarlequin.com or upon request from the Reader Service. From time to time we make our lists of customers available to reputable firms who may have a product or service of interest to you. If you would prefer we not share your name and address, please check here. ☐

LISUS07

Love Inspired ®
SUSPENSE

TITLES AVAILABLE NEXT MONTH

Don't miss these four stories in August

MURDER BY MUSHROOM by Virginia Smith
Cozy mystery

At the church potluck, Jackie Hoffner's casserole *killed*–
literally, unfortunately for the late Mrs. Farmer. Caught in the
police searchlights, Jackie would have to rely on handsome
Trooper Dennis Walsh and some snooping church ladies to
uncover who had cooked up the scheme to frame her.

CAUGHT REDHANDED by Gayle Roper

When Merry Kramer discovered a body while on her morning
jog, she wondered whether danger would ever stop following
her. She thought she knew the killer, but if she was unable to
prove what she had found out, was it worth risking her life or
losing her wonderful fiancé?

HIDE IN PLAIN SIGHT by Marta Perry
The Three Sisters Inn

The Amish countryside may have been a peaceful escape to
craftsman Cal Burke, but returning city girl Andrea Hampton
felt only its bitter memories. Family secrets, once bound
tight, began unraveling with an attack on her sister and with
the neighbors' new hostility. Relying on Cal, Andrea had to
get to the truth quickly–her life depended on it.

SCARED TO DEATH by Debby Giusti

A frantic call from a dying friend left Kate Murphy embroiled
in a sinister black-market deal and in danger of sharing her
friend's fate. Widower Nolan Price was full of secrets, but
joining forces with the single father was Kate's only hope to
survive.

LISCNM0707